The
Turf-Cutter's
Donkey

PATRICIA LYNCH

POOLBEG

FOR CHILDREN

First Published 1934
This edition published 1988 by
Poolbeg Press Ltd
123 Baldoyle Industrial Estate
Dublin 13, Ireland

Reprinted 1989
Reprinted May 1995
New edition reprinted 1998
Reprinted December 1998

© Estate of Patricia Lynch 1988

The moral right of the author has been asserted.

The Publishers gratefully acknowledge the support of The Arts Council.

A catalogue record for this book is available from the British Library.

ISBN 1 85371 808 4

Cover illustration by Peter Hanan
Cover design by Poolbeg Group Services Ltd
Printed by The Guernsey Press Ltd,
Vale, Guernsey, Channel Islands.

Contents

Contents

1

Eileen and Seamus meet the tinkers

ileen and Seamus lived in a cabin just beyond the crossroads at the edge of the great bog. The cabin was so low and the thatch so covered with grass and daisies, that a stranger would never have found it only that the walls were whitewashed.

Their father was a turf-cutter, but he knew so many songs to sing and so many tunes to whistle that he hadn't a deal of time for turf-cutting. Then there were the wet days and the cold days, as well as the holidays and the Sundays when it wasn't possible to work. But they had a grand little red cow from Kerry, an elegant pink pig in a neat, tidy sty, when the creature would stay there, and any number of hens and chickens, so they didn't do too badly.

Their mother made lace, beautiful lace – moss roses, shamrocks, and butterflies joined by a network of fine chains. When she had finished a piece she sold it on Fair Day at the town on the other side of the flat-topped mountain.

Round the cabin were piles of turf where the children played. The road ran past their home, right across the bog; and that was where they loved to be. In winter it was wild and bleak, but in summer it was white with canavan, the lovely bog-cotton, and the golden flags grew in the pools. There were treacherous green patches and holes so deep there was no bottom to them, but there were paths for those who knew, and trickling streams, and the wind which blew over it was fragrant.

Eileen and Seamus loved watching their father cut the soft brown turf with his slane, the long, sharp, cutting spade, and spread the oblong sods out to dry. First he piled them in threes, each leaning against the others so that the air could get all round them. Then they were gathered in heaps, and when they were quite dry they had to be loaded on carts and taken down to the great stack by the canal. Once a week a barge came and carried the turf away. Sometimes the captain allowed the children to travel with him as far as the lock, and Seamus made up his mind that when he was a man he would live on a barge and go all over the country instead of staying in a cabin, which never went anywhere.

'If only we had a little donkey!' said Eileen. 'I would love a little grey donkey! He could carry us to school and back, drag our turf home whenever we wanted some, and we could build him a grand little house with sods of turf.'

'And where would the likes of us be getting a donkey?' asked Seamus.

One morning they helped their father load the cart, said good-bye to their mother, to Big Fella the dog, and Rose the cat, and set off down to the canal. Eileen had a sore toe, so she sat on top of the turf while her father pulled and Seamus pushed.

It was a bright, sunshiny day, and Eileen was sorry when she saw how hot and red they were.

'If only we had the tiniest little donkey!' she said to herself. 'A little grey donkey!'

And she longed for that donkey more than she had ever longed for anything before.

At last they came to the canal.

The turf-cutter sat down to rest, for there was all the day before him for work, while Eileen and Seamus took the road to school.

But Eileen's sore toe hurt her so much that she limped.

'We'll never get to school at this rate of going!' exclaimed Seamus. 'Stand on this stone, Eileen, put your arms around my neck and I'll give you a piggy-back!'

Eileen stood up on the stone, but instead of putting her arms around her brother's neck, she pointed along the path.

'Look, Seamus! Look at the dotey little teapot!'

Seamus looked and there, shining and gleaming in every dent of it, was a battered silver teapot, no bigger than a breakfast cup!

He was so surprised he stood there staring, but Eileen jumped down from the stone and picked up the little teapot.

The lid was fastened securely and was tied to both the spout and the handle with a stout piece of string. As Seamus tried to untie the knots a great uproar came from a clump of trees at the bend of the road.

They heard the shouts of men and women, the screams of children, the barking of dogs, and, worst of all, the sound of a stick beating someone.

Eileen turned pale. Seamus clasped the teapot tightly.

'It's the tinkers!' whispered Eileen.

'Don't make a sound!' said Seamus softly. 'We'll take the path up the mountain and they'll never set eyes on us.'

He went first and Eileen, forgetting her sore toe, followed as quickly as she could. They were so nervous that they tripped over brambles, crushed dried twigs underfoot, and sent stones clattering down the mountain, but none of these sounds could be heard because of the tinkers' clamour.

Suddenly Seamus stopped. Through a gap in the bushes they could see right down into the tinkers' encampment.

A cart with a broken wheel was propped on a log. The tinkers were preparing to leave and the cart was loaded with their saucepans and kettles, while a bony horse stood in the shafts.

Some of the tinkers were searching among the bushes, others stood arguing, while a tall, ragged man, with a bushy black beard and a bright yellow handkerchief twisted about his head, was making a speech. At the end of every sentence he brought down a big stick on the back and sides of a donkey which was fastened to a tree.

The children had never seen such a thin, miserable donkey before. It did not move even when it felt the stick, but stood still, its head hanging down, its long ears folded over each other. Its tail was like a bit of cord, and its mane was all worn away.

'Oh, the poor donkey!' cried Eileen, bursting into tears. 'The poor little donkey!'

At that moment all the tinkers stopped their noise and Eileen's voice could be heard quite distinctly.

Some of the tinkers peered into the trees, others looked along the path, but the tall man stared straight up at the children.

'Come down along here out of that!' he roared.

The children turned and ran – the other way. As Seamus darted between the bushes, the sun gleamed on the silver teapot he still carried.

'After him!' cried the tall tinker. 'He's stolen our pot!'

Seamus laughed. He and Eileen were the best runners for miles around. The tinkers could never catch them! But as he laughed Eileen knocked her sore toe against a rock and, with a scream of pain, fell on her knees.

Seamus stopped and pulled her up.

'We must hide!' he said.

But what was happening to the tinkers?

The quiet donkey, with a sudden tug, broke the rope which fastened it to the tree. As the tall man who had been beating it, ordered the tinkers to follow the children, it gave a plunge, kicked up its heels, sent the tinkers tumbling over one another, and rushed up the hill-side.

As it passed, Seamus caught the broken rope and sprang on its back, while Eileen scrambled up behind.

Raising his hand above his head, Seamus flung the silver teapot towards the tinkers.

'Take the pot!' he shouted. 'We'll keep the donkey!'

2
The Magic pool

p the hill went the little grey donkey, with Eileen and Seamus clinging to its back.

There were paths round the hill but none of them went to the top, for it was very high and steep. But the donkey scrambled over rocks, and forced its way through brambles and bushes until the children's clothes were torn to flitters and Seamus began to wonder would they have any skin at all left on them!

'Won't it be grand if we get right to the top!' thought Eileen, peeping over her brother's shoulder.

'I do wish I could get off!' exclaimed Seamus as a bramble caught him by the leg and scratched, scratched, scratched!

At once the donkey stood still, put down its head, kicked up its heels, and sent Eileen and Seamus flying through the air.

They came down on a bed of springy heather. They bounced, rolled over, then lay still.

'That's a real bold donkey!' said Seamus crossly.

The donkey turned round, looked at Seamus, and

twitched his long ears.

'I'm sure he meant no harm!' Eileen said quickly, and the donkey looked away again.

The sun was blazing down on them. Everywhere bees were busy among the heather, sucking out the honey and filling their little satchels.

'What a grand place for a picnic!' exclaimed Seamus.

'Oh dear, I'm so hungry!' sighed Eileen. 'And I've lost my lunch!'

So had Seamus. They sat watching the little grey donkey, who was steadily eating his way through a clump of thistles. Suddenly he put down his head, flapped his ears and kicked up something from the grass.

'Oh!' cried Eileen, as a neat little packet flopped on her lap.

'Hooray!' shouted Seamus, as another package hit him on the shoulder.

'I thought I dropped my lunch just when we got on the donkey!' whispered Eileen.

So did Seamus, but these packets looked exactly like those their mother had given them when they left home.

Eileen opened hers. Inside was an apple cake, round and brown and crisp, with powdered sugar glistening on it.

Seamus opened his. He had a big piece of meat-pie – thick with jelly.

'I suppose they are meant for us!' wondered Eileen, looking timidly at the little grey donkey, for their packets had contained only a dry wedge of soda bread each.

Seamus didn't answer. He broke his piece of meat-pie into two and handed one to Eileen

They had never in all their lives tasted such lovely pie. When the last bit of jelly melted in their mouths, Eileen shared out the apple-cake.

'I think he's a real nice little donkey!' declared Eileen.

'Where's he going now, I wonder!' said Seamus.

The little grey donkey was slowly moving away from them. He had his head down and he kept on eating, so that the children could see only two big ears, for the heather and the bracken rose up between them.

'We've never been here before and we mustn't get lost!' exclaimed Seamus. 'Come along, Eileen. We'll go with him! Look – here's the way!'

They squeezed between two rocks which stood up tall and straight like a gateway.

Ahead of them was the donkey, eating away so hard that he had cleared a path which the children were able to follow easily.

But though as the donkey went on, he broke off long tough brambles all stiff with prickles, bit great mouthfuls of thick coarse grass, and they could hear his teeth crunch, crunch, crunch, Eileen and Seamus could not catch up to him.

'I've never seen a donkey eat so much in all my life!' cried Seamus.

'The poor little fellow was so thin! I'm sure he must have been starving!' Eileen whispered, for she did not want to hurt the donkey's feelings.

'He isn't thin now!' muttered Seamus.

Seamus was right. Every mouthful the donkey grew fatter. They could no longer see his ribs. He was round and smooth like a barrel. Even his tail was growing big and handsome.

Suddenly he began to run. Seamus ran too, pulling Eileen along with him.

At the end of the path made by the donkey they could

see a smooth circle of grass. Out into this he ran, flinging himself down and rolling over and over in delight.

'Seamus!' gasped Eileen, scarcely able to speak for excitement. 'We've found the magic pool!'

The turf-cutter had told his children of the pool on the hill-top, which was never dry even in the hottest weather.

Many had set out to find it, though few had succeeded, for those who wished as they looked into it, could see if their wishes would come true.

The pool was quite round. Butterflies of every size and colour, from tiny blue chalk butterflies to great purple emperors, fluttered over it and, as the children drew near, they saw the gaily coloured wings reflected in the water so that it seemed filled with flowers.

At one side a little water-rat sat washing his whiskers. He gave a sharp glance at Seamus, then dived into his hole under the bank.

'He's afraid you'd throw a stone at him!' said Eileen. 'But you wouldn't do that, would you, Seamus?'

Seamus knew Eileen hated him to be cruel and he thought her the best sister in all the four provinces of Erin, so he answered promptly: 'There aren't any stones here! But even if there were I wouldn't throw one!'

As he spoke, out came the water-rat and sat there looking at them.

Eileen thought him the prettiest little fellow she had ever seen. She admired his bright eyes, his furry head, his shiny nose.

'Oh, Seamus, if only he'd come to live in the pool by the bridge. We'd see him every day then!'

'I thought you wanted a donkey more than anything

else in the world!' exclaimed Seamus.

Eileen nodded her head very wisely.

'So I did! But we have a donkey now. At least, I suppose he's ours!'

'Of course he's ours! Didn't I give the tinkers the silver teapot?' demanded Seamus.

'We didn't see them pick it up. I wish I knew if they've found it!' sighed Eileen.

Now Seamus was just wishing he could go to Dublin on the turf-boat. But Eileen had spoken first. The water-rat beat the water with his tail until it was as clear as glass.

The two children knelt side by side and gazed into the pool, while the little grey donkey came and looked over their heads.

As the water became still they saw, very dimly at first, a picture of the tinkers' encampment. Gradually it became so distinct that they almost believed they were looking down upon the camp itself.

There was the cart – there the scattered fire, and there was the tall, dark chief marching up and down, clenching his fists and shaking his beard.

The little grey donkey shivered and squeezed closer to Eileen.

'They haven't found the teapot!' she murmured, as one by one they saw the tinkers coming back, looking very disappointed.

'That's not our fault!' said Seamus.

'Look! They're going away!' cried Eileen.

First went the chief. Then came the cart with all the little tinkers sitting on top of the pots and kettles, while the women tinkers pushed and pulled.

The men tinkers still searched as they went, lifting up

brambles, poking among the bracken with sticks, and turning over heaps of dead leaves.

Slowly the picture faded until the pool was quite clear again and the butterflies' wings were reflected in it once more.

'Hooray!' cried Seamus. 'I hope they never come back!'

'Hee-haw! Hee-haw!' laughed the little grey donkey, opening his mouth as wide as he could, while the water-rat, startled at such a noise, darted into his hole and left only the tiniest tip of his tail sticking out.

'But I do wish I knew where the teapot has got to!' complained Eileen.

3

What the teapot held

hat's not fair!' exclaimed Seamus indignantly. 'You've had one wish!'

He saw the rat waving his tail to and fro and pushed Eileen away so that she could not look into the water as the colours left it.

'I wish I could see will I ever get to Dublin on a turf-barge!' he said quickly.

But Eileen whispered her wish at the same time, and there in the pool they saw a confused picture – a battered silver teapot, a barge piled high with turf, mixed up with tinkers – old ones, young ones, and the reflection of their own two faces looking up at them.

'You've spoiled it all!' cried Seamus. 'And now we can't wish again!'

Eileen felt ashamed of herself.

'I only did it for fun!' she stammered.

Seamus marched away from the pool with his hands in his pockets. He didn't know where he was going, but he wanted to punish Eileen by frightening her.

He walked so quickly that in a moment he was hidden by the tall bracken.

'Seamus!' called Eileen. 'Do come back! I'm dreadfully sorry!'

But Seamus did not answer.

Eileen ran across the grassy circle after him and plunged into the bracken. There was no path, the big stems stood up like spears and she could not force her way through.

She stood on tiptoe and tried to see above the curling tips of the bracken fronds; but she wasn't tall enough, and her sore foot which hadn't bothered her for a long time began to hurt again.

She stood still, wondering which direction to take. A drop of rain splashed on her nose and, looking up, she saw great clouds travelling across the sky.

Eileen hated being alone, but she hated storms still more.

'Seamus! Seamus! Do come back! I'm frightened!' she cried, as the raindrops fell thick and fast.

The bracken was pushed to right and left and there was, not Seamus, but the little grey donkey!

Catching hold of one long ear, Eileen clambered on his back and looked around.

The rain was so heavy that she could see nothing but the tops of the bracken lying flat under the downpour.

There was no sign of Seamus, and she could no longer see the Wishing Pool.

The donkey made his way out of the bracken and began carefully to pick a path down the hill-side.

Eileen thought of Seamus left behind in the storm and forgot to be afraid.

'Little grey donkey!' she said. 'Find Seamus! I can't go without him.'

The donkey lifted up his head and hee-hawed as loudly as ever he could.

This time there came an answering shout, and Eileen saw Seamus running down to them.

He was dripping wet, and his knee was bruised where he had fallen down.

The little grey donkey scarcely waited for Seamus to climb up behind Eileen before he again started scrambling down the hill.

At first Eileen was so glad to have Seamus back that she never said a word. And Seamus was so glad to be with her that he kept silent too.

Besides, the rain beat in their faces, and talking was nearly as hard as seeing.

But when they came under the shelter of the trees at the bottom of the hill, Seamus felt he had to say something.

'I don't suppose we'll ever find the Wishing Pool again!' he said, shaking his head so that drops of water flew out of his hair.

'I never thought you'd run away and leave me, and we in a strange, wild place!' replied Eileen.

They might have had a real, serious quarrel then, only a great splash and a shout of terror startled them so that they nearly tumbled off the donkey's back.

It was lucky they held on tight, for where had the donkey brought them but to the canal bank, where it was very narrow!

The rain was not so heavy now, for the storm was almost over and the children could see about them.

Suddenly Seamus clutched Eileen by the arm.

'Don't make a sound!' he said. 'There are the tinkers!'

The tinkers were trudging along on the other side of the canal – they were wet and tired, and every few yards the broken wheel of their cart stuck in the mud so that they had to stop and lift it out.

Eileen felt sorry for them, they looked so miserable.

But what was that splashing about in the lock?

'Help!' came a choking cry.

'Oh, Seamus!' cried Eileen. 'It's a poor man fallen into the water!'

The tinkers were so concerned with their own troubles that they did not heed the cry for help, but Seamus slipped from the donkey's back and ran to the great wooden gate of the lock which separated the higher from the lower part of the canal.

After him came Eileen, and after Eileen trotted the little grey donkey.

The lock gate was shut and water was pouring down the smooth sides, so that whoever had fallen in had no way of getting up.

The water was so thick with foam that at first it was impossible to see who had cried for help. Then Eileen saw a gleam of yellow stuff, and a dark face lifted for a moment above the tossing spray.

'It's the big dark tinker!' she faltered, drawing back.

'I don't care who it is!' said Seamus. 'We must get him out!'

Around the donkey's neck hung the reins. Quickly Seamus unfastened them and, twisting one end around his body, lowered himself over the side of the lock.

The tinker's dark head appeared for a moment above the water. Seamus made a grab at him, but the man was so heavy that if the donkey's reins hadn't held firm they would both have been dragged under.

Half-blinded by the spray, Seamus twisted the reins round the tinker's arm and shouted to Eileen to lead the donkey away.

Slowly the boy and man rose out of the water. It was a great struggle for the little grey donkey, but he tugged with every bit of his strength and at last the tinker lay on the ground, his eyes closed and his arm swollen where the reins had tightened round it.

Seamus, Eileen, and the little grey donkey stood there looking down at the Tinker Chief. Presently his eyes opened and he glared up at them.

'You've got fat since I last saw you!' he said to the little donkey.

He unwound the rein from his arm and sat up.

The children had forgotten their fear of the tinkers. Now they remembered and wondered which way they should go. The little grey donkey, too, wagged his big ears and began to back away from the canal.

'You've saved me life, so I ought to be grateful!' said the Tinker Chief. 'Take the donkey and get out of this, before I change me mind!'

The children didn't wait to mount the little grey donkey, but the three of them set off running, and didn't stop until they came to the pool by the bridge.

The sky was still overcast, but in the water among the rushes there was a silver gleam.

Seamus looked up at the sky, hoping to see the sun.

'It's the teapot!' cried Eileen. 'And oh, Seamus! There's our water-rat. He brought it along to us!'

There sat the rat, washing his whiskers and mounting guard over the precious teapot.

Seamus had to wade out to get at it but, as he couldn't be any wetter than he was, that didn't matter.

The water-rat blinked at him with its bright little eyes, but never stopped washing its whiskers for one single moment.

As Seamus came back with the teapot under his arm, along the road came the turf-cutter, pushing his empty cart before him.

He was glad to be coming home, so he whistled away like a blackbird, and didn't he stare when he saw Eileen and Seamus and the state they were in, to say nothing of the little grey donkey!

'And what's the meaning of this?' he asked. 'And who made ye a present of that grand teapot?'

Eileen sat in the cart because she had a sore toe, the donkey pulled it and Seamus walked with his father and told him all their adventures.

He had just finished when they reached the cabin beyond the cross-roads at the edge of the bog.

There was the children's mother standing at the door, and her fingers working away at the loveliest piece of lace you ever saw.

She looked at the children all torn and muddy, and hugged them. She looked at the little grey donkey and stroked his long ears. Then she looked at the silver tea-pot which the turf-cutter put into her hands.

'Where in the wide world did you find my grand-mother's teapot that was stolen when I was a wee babby?' she asked.

So Seamus told his story all over again.

'And what's in the teapot?' asked Eileen.

'Gold sovereigns, to be sure!' replied her mother, cutting the strings which fastened the lid, with her black-handled bread-knife and emptying the shining coins out on the table.

'How did the tinkers get it?' Eileen wanted to know.

But no one could tell her that, and even if they could, they were all too busy counting the gold coins.

So they built another cottage with big windows and a fine thatched roof, with a grand stable for the little grey donkey.

And when the holidays came, they all went up to Dublin on the turf-barge and came back by the bus.

4

Boots on the wrong feet

eamus and Eileen were putting on their boots to go to the town at the other side of the flat-topped mountain.

They were to take a load of turf in the cart and bring back in exchange four pounds of tea, a stone of meal, a bag of sugar, a sack of flour, and a side of bacon.

Their mother sat at the table, making out the list.

'Put the basket under the seat!' she said. 'All the small packages can go in it. Let me see – currants and caraway seeds, salt and pepper, two ounces of plug for daddy, an ounce of peppermints for me, and two Peggy's legs!'

'They're for us!' said Seamus to Eileen.

The children were so excited they scarcely knew what they were doing, for it was market-day and the crowds of the world and all the fun you can imagine would be at the town.

Seamus sat on the floor, pulling on his boots. They felt very uncomfortable, and he couldn't make out what was wrong with them. But when he limped across the floor, Eileen burst out laughing.

'Oh, you silly!' she cried. 'Just look at your feet!'

Seamus looked down and saw what he had done. The

left boot was on his right foot and the right boot on his left foot. No wonder they hurt!

But he didn't like Eileen laughing at him.

'Anyway, my toes aren't sticking out like yours!' he said, flopping on the floor again and taking off his boots.

Eileen tried to hide her feet under her chair, but she was too late. Her mother had seen her toes poking from her boots.

'You can't go out like that!' she told Eileen. 'It's too wet and cold!'

Eileen was horrified. Not go to the Fair!

'Oh, please!' she coaxed. 'Do let me go. It isn't a bit cold today, and I'll be so careful. I won't walk in a single puddle!'

'You children are terribly hard on boots!' sighed their mother.

Eileen remembered how often she scrambled over the wall instead of going round to the gate. But it was trying to climb the big elm that had worn out the toes of her boots.

She looked so miserable that they all were sorry for her.

'If only you had another pair,' said her mother.

'Could I put a few nails in them?' suggested the turf-cutter.

Eileen held out her feet and he examined her boots. He shook his head.

'They're beyond me. I'm not much of a cobbler, and that's a fact. Never mind, Eileen. Seamus will take them with him to be mended, and tomorrow ye'll be runnin' round as if they were new.'

'I want to go to the Fair!' wailed Eileen.

'Listen now!' said her mother. 'I'll bake a grand little cake for your tea, and daddy will tell you a grand new story.'

But Eileen couldn't be comforted that way.

'I'd sooner go to the Fair than anywhere else in the world!' she declared.

Seamus felt he was to blame. If only he hadn't said anything, his mother mightn't have noticed.

'If Eileen stays in the cart, wouldn't that do?' he asked.

'Will you promise?' asked their mother.

'Oh, I will!' shouted Eileen, dancing round the kitchen. 'I won't move out of the cart, whatever happens!'

She was so afraid something else might come along to keep her at home, that she got up into the cart before Long Ears was out of his stable.

'Remember to tell the cobbler you want the boots to come home in,' the turf-cutter reminded them, as he held the gate open for the cart to pass through.

'Don't forget you must stay in the cart, Eileen!' called their mother.

'I do wish the summer would come again, so that we could go without any horrid boots!' thought Eileen to herself.

Seamus cracked the whip, and away trotted Long Ears. The wind was cold, but the sky was blue and every puddle shone and ruffled. Eileen was so happy, she sang at the top of her voice. Seamus marched ahead whistling, and Long Ears followed him as though he had nothing to pull but the cart and Eileen.

They crossed the bridge and waved their hands to the water-rat who was peeping from his hole to find out what all the noise was about.

The road began to rise and Long Ears slowed down, for after all he had a load of turf as well as Eileen to pull.

'Seamus! Wouldn't it be fine if we could get some primroses?' called Eileen. 'Do watch out!'

'It's too early,' Seamus told her.

'But this isn't an ordinary mountain!' explained Eileen. 'Almost anything could happen here!'

At that moment Long Ears pulled the cart quickly to one side of the road and Eileen caught a glimpse of something small and brown scuttling across and diving in among the bushes.

'Seamus!' she called in a whisper. 'Seamus! Did you see?'

Seamus was lifting some withered bracken to see if the primroses were blooming yet and he hadn't seen anything.

'What was it?' he asked. 'A rabbit?'

Eileen didn't answer. She was staring up the mountain. Seamus ran back to her.

'What did you see? Do tell me!'

Eileen bent down and whispered in his ear. 'I do believe it was a leprechaun.'

'You are a little duffer!' exclaimed Seamus scornfully.

Eileen pointed up the mountain. 'Look, Seamus! Look, quick! There he goes!'

Seamus looked and started with amazement.

In and out among the bushes, bending low, ran a little man, wearing a leather apron and a long peaked cap. His beard, which was as long as himself, was carefully tucked into his belt to keep it tidy, and in one hand he held the tiniest shoe the children had ever seen.

He was searching in the grass, under the bushes, all around the trees, in the crevices of the rocks.

'Wait here!' whispered Seamus. 'I'm going to catch him!'

Treading as lightly as he could, up the mountain went

Seamus, leaving Eileen and Long Ears at the side of the road.

5

Catching a leprechaun

ileen was always wanting to hear stories, but Seamus thought himself far too big to be listening to nonsense about leprechauns and the like.

He wished now that Eileen had come with him, for he couldn't remember what he should do with the leprechaun when he had caught him.

Now Seamus had a great opinion of himself!

'That leprechaun's only a little chap! I'll soon settle him!' he said to himself. 'I won't let him go until he's given me his pot of gold. That's all that matters!'

And on he ran.

While Seamus kept to the path he mounted quickly. But as he came near the leprechaun he was afraid of being seen, so he slipped in among the rocks and brambles.

He had to go carefully, for the ground was strewn with loose stones which gave way beneath his feet.

He could hear the little man sighing as he searched:

'Oh dear! Oh dear! Where did I drop it?'

Seamus was so occupied in watching him that he did not notice where he was treading. A bramble caught his stocking and, trying to shake himself free, he kicked a stone.

It went tumbling down the mountain-side, bounding from rock to rock and making such a clatter that the leprechaun sprang into the air with fright, while Seamus stood absolutely still, not daring to move.

'What a shame!' he thought. 'I'm sure to be discovered now!'

'What was that?' exclaimed the little brown man. 'Oh, dear! Oh, dear! What can that be!'

He turned so quickly in every direction that he spun round on one heel. His beard flew loose, his apron fluttered like a flag. But he kept a fast hold of the shoe he was carrying.

The leprechaun looked so funny that Seamus began to laugh. He tried not to. He pressed his lips tightly, he clenched his teeth, he put his hands over his face, but at last – out came his laughter, spluttering and gurgling.

The little man had been frightened before, now he was terrified. As the strange sound was carried by the wind up the mountain, he leaped into the air and came down trembling and panting just beside Seamus!

'What luck!' thought the boy, hardly able to believe his good fortune, and putting out his hand, he caught the leprecnaun by the arm.

'Oh! Oh! Oh!' screamed the tiny fellow, kicking and struggling. 'Let me go! Let me go!'

Seamus almost did let go, but not quite.

He was sorry that the leprechaun was so frightened, but he was determined not to let go until he had found at least one pot of gold.

'Don't be scared,' he said gently. 'I'm not hurting you, and I'll set you free the moment you show me where you keep your gold.'

The leprechaun stared up at him and became quite still.

'Why, it's Seamus!' he said. 'Eileen's big brother. I'm very pleased to meet you, Seamus!'

Seamus opened his eyes as big as saucers; he was so surprised to hear the leprechaun talk like this.

'Do you know Eileen?' he asked. 'She never told me!'

The little man smiled and put one finger against the side of his long, pointed nose.

'Ho! Ho! Ho! I know her and she's never seen me. But she could tell you all about me. It's a great pity she isn't here. We could have a grand talk together!'

Seamus thought it would be a good thing to have Eileen with him, for she certainly did know all about leprechauns and their ways. But he was afraid to move.

'Eileen!' he called. 'Eileen! Come up here, quickly. It's most important.'

Eileen heard him, but she remembered her promise.

'I can't come!' she called back. 'I must stay in the cart!'

Her voice floated faintly up the mountain-side.

'Bother!' muttered Seamus, not knowing what to do. 'We'll have to go down to her!'

The mountain-side was so steep and rough he needed both hands to descend safely, and he stood there, feeling vexed and puzzled.

'Show me where she is!' said the leprechaun. 'Me eyes are not all they should be. It's the terrible job I have, cobbling from morning till night! You'd pity me!'

'Why wouldn't you mend Eileen's boots for her?' asked Seamus, laughing. 'Look! There she is. Down by the red rock, sitting up in the donkey-cart!'

He stepped forward to show where his sister waited.

His foot slipped and, flinging out his arms to save himself, he opened his hand and let the leprechaun go.

The little man dropped lightly on a heap of dried bracken. There was a flash of brown in the sunlight, a scurry among the froachan bushes, and the leprechaun was gone!

Seamus stared about him. How disappointed he was!

'I am a stupid!' he thought regretfully. 'Just think of the time we could have at the Fair if only I hadn't let go!'

A low chuckle came from behind him and he swung round. Another sounded on the right and, scrambling on his hands and knees, he pounced that way. He heard it above him, he heard it below, until every bush and rock seemed to be laughing at him.

Who was that singing?

> 'Would you find my hoard of gold?
> When you catch me – DON'T LET GO!
> I am wise and very old,
> Every dodge and trick I know.
> Seamus! Seamus! now you'll know –
> Next time you catch me – DON'T LET GO!'

Seamus flushed.

'I don't think I'll tell Eileen what happened. She'd think me such a silly!' he said to himself as he went slowly and carefully down the mountain.

T—B

6

A hammer of gold

While Seamus was having his adventure Eileen sat in the cart, looking about her. The snow had gone and the sun was shining but the wind made her shiver.

Seamus and the leprechaun were out of sight, and though Eileen kept very still, she could not hear a sound.

She wrapped herself in the rug which was folded on the seat and, bending down, pulled a sack over Long Ears, for he hated the cold too.

'Seamus is sure to come back with a big pot full up of gold. The leprechaun will never best him,' she told the little donkey proudly.

But oh! it was tormenting having to sit still while Seamus was having such a wonderful time!

Eileen sang to herself for company, while her eyes searched the bank, hoping to find the pale yellow of primrose flowers showing through the grass.

The bracken, brown and withered, lay in dead heaps. The bushes crouched bare against the earth, and the trees stood up black against the pale blue sky. Everything looked cold and cheerless. Even the sunshine had no warmth and Eileen began to be impatient for Seamus to return.

'Maybe it wasn't a leprechaun at all,' she thought sadly, looking up at the dark mountain.

It was then she heard Seamus calling her!

'What shall I do?' wondered Eileen. 'He doesn't sound frightened. It must be that he wants me to help him find the leprechaun and he's forgotten I promised not to stir from the cart.'

She called back and sat listening anxiously.

What was that queer singing coming down from the mountain? Eileen couldn't make out the words, but she felt sure the sound had something to do with Seamus.

'If he is in trouble I've a right to go and help him!' she decided.

Throwing off the rug, Eileen stood up in the cart. Suddenly she cried out.

In the long grass a little way up the mountain she saw a gleam of yellow!

Quickly she clambered out of the cart and forced her way through the tangled grass and brambles.

There it was! A yellow gleam, as though the sun was blazing through the trees.

Eileen fell on her knees and pressed back the grass.

'Seamus!' she called, her voice trembling with excitement. 'Seamus! Do come quickly. You can't imagine what I've found!'

Not primroses, but a tiny hammer with a handle of white, carved wood, and a head of shining gold!

She picked it up. Though so small, it was perfectly made.

'I do believe it's the leprechaun's hammer!' whispered Eileen. 'Wouldn't I love to see him make shoes for the Good People with it!'

The grass was soaking where the snow had melted without sinking into the ground. Eileen's stockings, her coat, her old broken boots were wet. Her teeth were chattering with cold, but there she knelt admiring the little hammer and forgetting everything else.

'But what will the leprechaun do without it?' she thought.

'That's my hammer!' screamed a shrill, angry voice above her.

Eileen sprang to her feet and peered up through the tangle of bush and bracken.

The leprechaun was glaring down at her, shaking his fists and dancing with rage.

He looked very comical, but Eileen didn't laugh. All her life she had longed to see the Good People, and now she had the luck to be quite close to one.

'I'll bring it up to you!' she said eagerly. 'I just picked it up and I never meant to keep it. I knew it must belong to you!'

The leprechaun watched her timidly as she climbed up to him. He remembered how Seamus had caught him and he feared that Eileen might want to get his gold too.

But Eileen was so pleased to meet him, that she did not dream of wanting anything from him.

As she came near him he got behind a rock and prepared to run if she tried to grab him.

'He isn't as big as I am,' thought Eileen. 'And the poor little fellow; he's quite scared.'

'Here is your hammer, Mr. Leprechaun!' she said, making a very polite bow and holding out the hammer. 'It's the prettiest thing I've ever seen and I'm delighted I found it for you. But what a beautiful shoe that is under your arm. You must be a terribly clever shoemaker!'

The leprechaun was charmed with her praise.

'Why, it's yerself, Eileen!' he exclaimed, pretending he hadn't recognized her before. 'I might have known you wouldn't play tricks on one of *us*!'

He reached out and took the hammer. As his fingers closed on the handle he sprang back, but Eileen did not move.

'Will you please let me see you making a shoe?' she asked coaxingly.

The leprechaun was puzzled. He had never been asked such a favour before. He looked to the right. He looked to the left. He did not know what to say!

'You're a real kind little girl!' he said at last. 'I'll see what I can do for you. Let me think now. Let me think hard!'

He held his chin in his hand and thought hard. Eileen held her breath as she watched him anxiously.

Unluckily, as he opened his mouth to speak, a rock loosened by Seamus came rolling down. Eileen jumped one way. The leprechaun leaped the other.

Eileen slipped on the wet grass and sat down suddenly. 'Have you made up your mind yet?' she asked hurriedly. She was afraid the interruption might have annoyed the leprechaun.

There was no answer. She looked at the spot where the leprechaun had been standing. There were the marks of tiny feet in the mud. But there was no leprechaun.

Where had he jumped? She peered under the bushes. She lifted up the heaps of bracken. She stared up at the trees.

Stones bounded down the mountain-side, so that Eileen had to shelter under a rock and Long Ears hee-hawed warningly.

'Seamus!' cried Eileen. 'Do be careful. You're sending piles of stones down on top of us!'

Seamus strode along. He looked bad-tempered. He frowned when he saw his sister and the state she was in.

'Oh, Seamus!' said Eileen reproachfully. 'He was just thinking would he let me see him making shoes!' Seamus was disappointed about his own ill-luck. He couldn't be expected to know that Eileen had talked with the same leprechaun.

'Aren't you the tiresome girl!' he scolded. 'Didn't you promise to stay in the cart? And look at the sight you are! Everyone at the Fair will think I've brought a scarecrow with me. And won't you catch it when we get home!'

'But Seamus,' protested Eileen, 'you called me, and then I found the leprechaun's hammer!'

'What!' shouted Seamus. 'You've got his hammer? He'll never be able to do without it. Why didn't you tell me? We'll make him give us pots of gold in exchange for it. Where is it? Show it to me!'

'I gave it to him,' confessed Eileen, wondering if she had been very foolish.

'Gave it to him?' echoed Seamus. 'And didn't you make him promise to do anything for it?'

She shook her head.

'I asked him to let me see him making a shoe, and he was thinking hard about it when that big rock came rolling down. I tumbled over, and when I got up he was gone.'

'You're the silliest girl I've ever known!' exclaimed Seamus scornfully. 'I'm ashamed to have you for my sister!'

'He was so little and he looked so frightened!' cried Eileen. 'And I don't care what you say. I'm glad I gave him back his hammer!'

While they were talking, the children had been scrambling back to the road. As they reached the level ground beside the cart, Long Ears put his head on Eileen's shoulder and rubbed her cheek with his nose.

'Hee-haw! Hee-haw!' he said consolingly.

Eileen flung her arms round his neck.

'I do believe Long Ears thinks I'm right!' she declared triumphantly. 'And he's the wisest donkey in the world!'

Seamus cocked his nose in the air. He was still annoyed with Eileen and, what was worse, he was annoyed with himself. After all, he had caught the leprechaun and he had tried his best to get the little fellow's gold, while Eileen hadn't bothered.

They got into the cart.

'Oh! Oh!' screamed Eileen. 'My toes are pricking. Oh! They do hurt!'

At once Seamus forgot his anger.

'Show me, Eileen,' he said. 'Maybe you've run a thorn into your foot. I'll pull it out for you!'

Eileen held out her two feet.

'It's the both of them,' she told her brother. 'Oh, Seamus! See what's happened!'

Seamus knelt there with his eyes nearly popping from his head.

When they started from home Eileen's toes had been sticking out from her boots. Now the ragged ends had been tucked in, a patch of new leather had been put on each boot, neatly sewn with tiny gold stitches on top, and there were little gleaming nails in the soles!

'The leprechaun has made them better than the best boots I've ever had, the dote!' cried Eileen.

Seamus did not speak. He looked beneath the seat. He lifted the rug. He got out of the cart and searched underneath that. He looked up the road. He looked down the road. He stared at the rocks, the bushes, the trees on each side, but never a glimpse of the leprechaun did he catch!

Silently he climbed back into the cart.

'We needn't go to the cobbler's now!' said Eileen. 'And I can have a grand time at the Fair. Seamus! Would you ever have believed that such a little man could be so clever? To mend my boots and me sitting here! And indeed, there aren't many girls in the whole of Ireland, I should think, who've had their boots mended by a leprechaun!'

Oh, she was proud!

At last Seamus found his voice.

'We'd best be getting on to the Fair,' he said. 'Gee-up, there! Stir yourself, Long Ears!'

And on trotted the little grey donkey.

7

At the fair

As Long Ears drew the cart along the last bit of the path by the flat-topped mountain, the children could see the main road lying below them.

How crowded it was! There were men and boys driving cows and pigs and sheep, with dogs running and barking around them. There were carts loaded with hens in crates, and ducks in low, flat baskets; carts loaded with lambs and with bonhams, with winter cabbages piled high and the frost still on them. There were women carrying baskets of eggs, women pushing little carts loaded with apples, with oranges.

Best of all – there were pedlars and ballad-singers!

Every single one of them made a noise, and all the noises mingled into one big noise.

'Hurray!' cried Eileen. 'Now we are going to the Fair!'

'Hee-haw!' sang out Long Ears, for he liked a bit of fun just as much as Eileen, and all the donkeys pulling carts on the road answered him.

But Seamus sat silent and said never a word.

He wasn't a greedy boy, but he couldn't help thinking what fine spending there would have been in even the littlest pot of the leprechaun's hoard of gold.

'Here we are,' he thought sadly, 'going to the Fair, and all we'll have is two Peggy's legs. It's a shame, so it is!'

'Wouldn't you whistle a tune, Seamus?' asked Eileen. 'Then I could sing, and Long Ears would march along grand and quick.'

Suddenly Seamus was ashamed of his ill-temper. He made up his mind not to be cross any longer.

'Tim Quinlan was teaching me a fine, new tune,' he told his sister. 'I don't know it all, and you mustn't try to sing it or you'll put me out.'

Eileen was delighted to have him friendly again.

'I'll sit quiet and listen,' she promised. 'I do love a tune.'

Seamus tilted his cap to the back of his head and stuck out his lips.

Eileen watched him eagerly. She was always trying to whistle, but she could never make anything but a humming noise.

Seamus swelled his cheeks, his face got red, he frowned and stamped his feet impatiently, but no sound came from his pursed lips.

'Can't you remember that tune?' asked Eileen. 'Never mind. Whistle one I know. Then I can sing.'

Seamus would not give up. He tried again. He took a deep breath. He blew softly. He blew hard. But never a bit of difference did it make.

Seamus, who knew almost twenty tunes, couldn't get out a single note.

They were in the crowd now, and a small, ragged man, with an untidy beard, who was driving a little white pig with a string tied to one of its hind legs, looked up at the boy curiously.

'What ails the young lad?' he asked in a high, squeaky

voice.

A woman sitting up in her cart stared at the faces Seamus was making, and burst out laughing.

'Stir him up with the toe of your boot, girleen!' called the small ragged man.

Eileen turned to look at him, and knocked her brother with the toe of her boot.

At once Seamus began to whistle so clearly and loudly that the people in front of them and the people at the back of them, to say nothing of Long Ears, began marching in step, like soldiers.

Eileen was puzzled. She looked around for the small, ragged man. But he was gone!

No! There he was, with the wind blowing his beard backwards round his neck like a muffler. He and his pig were dodging in and out among the people, and it was the greatest of wonders that the string tied to the white pig's leg didn't trip someone up.

'He's mighty like the leprechaun,' thought Eileen.

She was just going to give Seamus a poke to make him look, when she changed her mind.

She wasn't sure, and it would be a pity to stop Seamus – and he whistling so grand, with all the people marching to his tune.

They reached the Fair Green in fine style.

Eileen jumped out first, without holding to the side of the cart or stepping on the wheel.

'I never jumped like that before,' she said to herself. 'It must be the way my boots are mended.'

'Hurry up, Seamus!' she called to her brother. 'We must get a good place for Long Ears.'

Seamus gave a start and blinked his eyes as if he had just woke up.

'I didn't know we were half-way here,' he muttered.

But he climbed down and began to lead Long Ears away.

Eileen meant to follow him, but at that moment a ballad-singer began calling to the people to gather round.

If there was one thing Eileen liked better than a new song, it was an old one.

She squeezed into the front of the crowd, while Seamus went off to the strip of grass under the trees by a high wall, where there was a grand waiting-place for horses and donkeys.

Seamus in all his life had never seen such a gathering. There were big ones, little ones. There were grey, brown, black, and white ones. There were some with the most elegant harness imaginable, and others with old collars and traces tied up with bits of string.

'But Long Ears is the best of the lot, isn't he, Eileen?' declared Seamus proudly, as the little grey donkey marched to the end of the row against a broken railing.

There was no answer, and Eileen was always so quick to praise Long Ears that the boy turned round in wonder.

To his amazement Eileen wasn't with him!

'Why didn't she keep by me?' cried Seamus. 'She'll get lost in that crowd, and she'll be frightened too.'

Forgetting, in his haste, to fasten Long Ears, Seamus ran back to where the stands and stalls and tents were surrounded by the noisy, pushing mob.

He looked for her where the pigs were being sold. He searched where the cows were mooing sadly to one another. He climbed up on the stand among the crates of fowls and ducks, and strained his eyes to catch sight of a little girl with grey eyes, brown hair and a red tammy.

'What shall I do if I can't find her?' Seamus asked

himself, and for him all the fun had gone out of the Fair.

He remembered now that they should have taken the cart to the dealers and got rid of the turf before coming on the Fair Green, but nothing seemed to matter to Seamus until he had found Eileen.

He wriggled and pushed his way along by the stalls.

'Fine oranges and apples, one penny each!' called a woman.

'Fizz drink, penny the glass!' was shouted at him, but Seamus scarcely paused to see it foaming in the tumblers.

He was so cold that the hot drinks, red and yellow, did tempt him; but he had no money, so he let himself be carried along by the crowd.

There were thick ham sandwiches piled up on white cloths. One woman was cutting and selling, as hard as she could, great wedges of hot apple-cake. Seamus sniffed the lovely spicy smell of the cloves as he passed on.

At another stall there were mugs of steaming coffee and freshly made soda bread, spread thickly with yellow butter.

He came to a stop by the fortune-teller, wondering if he dared ask her to find Eileen for him.

She was dressed in red, with a spotted yellow handkerchief tied over her dark hair.

Beside her was a big gilt cage full of pretty, green birds.

Seamus watched a girl giving money for a fortune.

The fortune-teller opened the door of the cage and thrust in a white wand. One of the birds hopped on it and the woman waved it gently over a box of small, folded papers, red, green, and yellow.

The bird picked one out, but instead of giving it to the girl, tossed it into the air.

The scrap of paper fell on Seamus's arm. He opened

it and saw in printed letters:

> 'Where the singers' voices rise,
> There you'll find Grey Eyes.'

'That's mine!' angrily cried the girl who had paid for a fortune, and she snatched it from Seamus before he could read any farther. 'If you want one, why don't you pay for it?'

'I haven't any money,' replied Seamus. 'And I don't want a fortune. I only want to know where my sister is. Please tell me,' he added, turning to the fortune-teller.

'I want none of your impidence,' she said crossly. 'Gwan out o' that!'

'Would you give a pot of gold, if you had it?' asked a voice at the boy's elbow.

Looking down Seamus saw a queer, small man with a long ragged beard, and a little white pig tucked under his arm.

Seamus had a feeling that he had seen the man before, but he couldn't think where.

'I'd give all the gold in the world, but I haven't a penny!' he replied.

The small, ragged man put his head on one side, stood on tiptoe, and sang in the boy's ear:

> 'Where the singers' voices rise,
> There seek little Grey Eyes.'

'You're making fun of me!' cried Seamus indignantly.

He turned away, because there were tears in his eyes and he was afraid someone might see them.

Suddenly he heard a cracked, shaky voice singing.

He could hear nothing more for the shouts of laughter

which came from the far side of the Green.

Then above the uproar rose a high, clear voice, singing the same song; but this time he could hear every word.

' 'Tis Eileen!' cried Seamus in delight. 'But what can she be doing, singing out here at the Fair?'

He tried to get to her, but everyone else was doing the same.

'What's the trouble?' asked a man who was pricing pigs.

' 'Tis an old, mad ballad-singer and his little girl,' replied the dealer in fowls and ducks, for he was high up on his stand and could see over the people's heads. 'The lads started tormentin' the old chap and the little one is taking his part, more power to her.'

'If only I could get to Eileen,' sighed Seamus. 'I'd teach them!' And he fought and struggled to get through the crowd.

'Don't you wish your boots had been mended by a leprechaun?' asked a squeaky voice.

Seamus started. There was the queer, small man with his white pig. He ducked under the boy's arm and got in front of him. Then he put down the pig, and with its little snout it worked a way among the people, which let the small man through and after him came Seamus.

Everyone in the crowd was pushing, but the little white pig, the small man, and Seamus pushed hardest of all; so they came at last, right into the centre.

There stood a very old ballad-singer, dressed in a long black coat that was split across the shoulders. On his head was a top-hat without a crown.

The singer's hair was long and bushy, and it stuck up out of the hat in a tangled mass. His grizzled beard grew out around his face, and in his hand he held a few song-sheets.

Many more sheets were trampled into the mud, and the poor singer stood with his mouth hanging open with fear, and not singing a word.

Never in all his life had Seamus seen such a miserable creature, but he scarcely noticed him, for there was Eileen, very white and frightened, but singing away like a lark.

Around them were gathered all the rough boys at the Fair. They pulled at the ballad-singer's coat and tore up his song-sheets.

Some of the people laughed, others cried out that it was a terrible shame; but not one of them interfered.

'Eileen!' shouted Seamus, the moment he set eyes on her. 'I've been searching everywhere for you!'

'Here's another of them!' yelled the wildest of the boys. 'Let's make the three sing together!'

Eileen gave a cry of joy and darted towards her brother, but without leaving go of the ballad-singer's hand.

The boys who were teasing the ballad-singer caught hold of Eileen and pulled her back.

Seamus jumped in front of her and clenched his fists.

'Out of the way!' he said, and gave the boy nearest him a push that sent him toppling.

'Good lad! Good lad!' cried several men in the crowd, and they elbowed themselves forward to help him.

But the bullies were all together. Seamus glanced this way and that. How could they escape?

'Jump high, Eileen. Jump high!' called a squeaky voice from the crowd.

Eileen caught Seamus by the hand.

'Jump!' she ordered. 'Jump!'

The boy he had knocked over caught him by the elbow.

'I'll teach you to push me!' he muttered, when to his amazement, Seamus gave a jump and a kick.

Once more the bully went sprawling. This time he did not attempt to get up, but lay stretched on his back, wondering if he were dreaming.

For Eileen, Seamus, and the ballad-singer rose lightly in the air, floated over the crowd, and disappeared behind the trees!

What a hullaballoo came from the people! Not one there, except maybe a small, ragged man with a white pig tucked under his arm, could believe his eyes.

'Did you see that?' asked one.

'Some smart laddy-boy playing a trick!' declared another.

Everyone wanted to explain, but no one believed what had happened.

The boy lying on the ground scrambled to his feet and rubbed his shoulder where Seamus had kicked him.

He stood staring up at the sky, until a man saw him and gave him a shaking.

'You young rascal! Making all this trouble!' he said angrily.

'It's my belief, boys and ballad-singers haven't any right to be on the Green at all!' declared a woman, wrapping her shawl closely round her. 'Between the screechings of the both of them the Fair isn't worth coming to at all. So it isn't!'

'Did ye see the way they lepped into the air?' asked the boy, rubbing his shoulder.

But no one listened to him.

Eileen, Seamus, and the ballad-singer came down on the ground with a bump.

'Let me get out of this!' exclaimed the singer. 'There's

magic and bewitching at the Fair today. A decent man's life isn't safe!'

And off he ran, his black coat flapping behind him.

'Seamus!' cried Eileen. 'You're real brave! And aren't these grand boots? Let's try another jump!'

'No!' replied Seamus. 'We might come down where we wouldn't want to be. I've had enough of this Fair. Besides, we haven't taken the turf to the Stores. We must do that and go home.'

He marched off across the grass to where he had left Long Ears and the cart.

Eileen, feeling very sad and disappointed, followed him slowly.

She saw Seamus pass along the line of donkeys and horses tethered under the trees. Half-way down he began to run and, wondering what was wrong, Eileen ran too.

When she came up with Seamus she found him standing still, looking puzzled and worried.

'What is the matter, Seamus?' she asked. 'And where is Long Ears?'

'That's just what I don't know!' replied the boy. 'I left him here and now he's gone. Look! There are the marks of his hoofs!'

'Did you tie him up?' asked Eileen, looking anxiously about.

'Don't ask silly questions!' snapped Seamus and, as he spoke, he remembered that he hadn't tied the little donkey at all. But who would expect Long Ears to go wandering away, just like an ordinary donkey?

'Someone must have stolen him!' cried Eileen. 'Oh, my poor Long Ears! What shall we do?'

They looked at the donkeys and horses, contentedly shaking up their nose-bags and munching steadily away.

If only Long Ears had been there too, how happy they would feel!

'It's all your fault,' grumbled Seamus. 'If you had stayed with me instead of listening to ballad-singers, this would never have happened.'

Indeed this was true, but when he saw tears coming into Eileen's eyes, Seamus couldn't go on blaming her.

'Never mind,' he said quickly, 'we'll search for Long Ears until we find him.'

'Suppose those bold boys have taken him,' suggested Eileen, looking scared.

'That couldn't be,' Seamus pointed out. 'They weren't near him. No! He must have wandered away.'

'How could Long Ears have wandered away when he was tied up?' Eileen wanted to know.

Seamus frowned, but he hated telling lies, so he owned up.

'When I found you weren't with me I was bothered, and I think I must have forgotten to fasten him.'

'Then it was my fault,' said Eileen sorrowfully. 'I shouldn't have stayed to hear the ballad-singer. And he wasn't worth listening to. He was the worst singer I ever heard! He didn't know a single song right through, and he had all the tunes mixed up.'

Seamus wasn't listening to her. He was staring in amazement along the path which led across the Fair Green to the town.

'Look at the robber marching off with Long Ears!' he exclaimed. 'After him, Eileen. After him!'

He dashed away. Eileen ran too, and because of her wonderful boots she passed him easily, though he was running his hardest.

Eileen reached the cart first and trotted beside it,

laughing.

'Seamus!' she called. 'He isn't a robber at all. He is helping us.'

'Hee-haw!' agreed Long Ears.

Seamus looked from Eileen to the small, ragged man perched up on the driver's seat and a little white pig sitting there beside him. He didn't know what to make of it at all.

'What happened to our turf?' demanded Seamus, going round to the back.

There wasn't a sod left, but, neatly piled behind the seat, he saw a bag of meal and a small sack of flour sitting on top of a side of bacon.

In the middle of the cart was a huge parcel tied in brown paper, with a written list pinned to it.

He read the list out aloud:

'4 lb. tea; 1 lb. currants; 2 oz. caraway seeds; 1 slab salt; 1 oz. best white pepper; 2 oz. best cut plug; 1 oz. extra strong peppermints; 2 Peggy's legs.'

On top of the parcel lay an envelope with Eileen's name on it.

'I don't understand,' began Seamus.

'I do!' Eileen interrupted. 'And I'd sooner have things happen this way than find all the pots of gold in the world.'

'He isn't a –' started Seamus, determined to finish speaking this time.

But a sudden fierce gale of wind swept down from the mountains and he had no chance to end what he was saying.

A badly fixed tent was caught up and went sailing away overhead like an enormous wild goose. An apple stall was turned upside down and the boys and girls went

racing to pick up the apples rolling over the grass. Dust
and straw and feathers flew through the air, hats and caps
danced, then stopped, then danced again, leading their
angry owners from one side of the Green to another.

Seamus laughed and laughed, it looked so comical.
Suddenly his cap gave a leap from his head and careered
away.

'Oh, oh, me best cap!' cried Seamus, and off he went
in pursuit.

The cap danced and swirled before Seamus as though
it had at least a dozen legs.

He ran and dodged. Just as he reached the cap it jerked
sideways and he had to turn so quickly that he tumbled
over.

'If it wasn't me best cap it could go where it pleased,'
thought Seamus, getting up and making a sudden spring.

The wind dropped as suddenly as it had risen. The cap
lay quite still and waited there for Seamus to pick it up.

He put it on his head and walked slowly back.

Eileen was sitting up in the driver's seat, looking delighted with herself.

Where was the small, ragged man with his white pig?
Seamus did not ask.

'Look, Seamus!' cried Eileen, making room beside her
on the seat.

Spread out on her lap were an envelope, a strip of
paper, two new half-crowns. On the strip of paper was
printed: 'Here's a little to go on with.'

'There's half a crown for me and half a crown for you,'
said Eileen. 'I've never had so much money in my life
before!'

'Is it real money?' asked Seamus suspiciously.

'Of course it is!' declared Eileen indignantly.

'Are you sure it's meant for us?' Seamus wanted to know.

'I know it is!' replied Eileen. 'Isn't my name on the envelope?'

'Then we'd better put Long Ears in the station yard and start having some fun!' decided Seamus. 'Five shillings isn't a pot of gold, but we'll do the best we can. Gee-up, Long Ears!'

Eileen and Seamus didn't say another word until the cart was safely backed into the station yard and Long Ears left on the sloping grassy bank near the signal-box

From there the little grey donkey could look over the hedge down at the Fair. He had plenty to eat and he was sheltered from the wind.

'What shall we do first?' asked Eileen as they jumped down the stone steps into the roadway.

'I saw some hot apple-cake over there,' replied Seamus. 'Let's have some of that and a big mug of tea each.'

'I love apple-cake!' declared Eileen. 'And I'm starved with the hunger. Had it sugar on top?'

'Heaps!' Seamus told her. 'And cloves inside. Then we'll go on the roundabouts!'

'And the swings!' added Eileen.

They hurried through the crowd and Eileen could smell hot apples and cloves, when Seamus stopped suddenly.

The small, ragged man with his white pig was standing beside the apple-cake woman, watching her cut her cakes and sprinkle them with white sugar.

He looked so hungry that Eileen felt sorry for him, but Seamus frowned.

'Now, how did he come here?' the boy wondered.

No one else noticed the small man and the pig, although they were in the way of the people crossing from the station to the stalls, and twice they were almost knocked over.

'Look!' whispered Eileen. 'That's the little man who took care of Long Ears and gave us our half-crowns. Let's buy him some apple-cake!'

Without waiting for Seamus to agree, she ran up to the small man.

'Would you like some apple-cake?' she asked.

The small man nodded his head backwards and forwards so quickly that Seamus wondered it didn't come off. While the white pig sat up on his hind legs and grunted.

'I wonder if a pig can eat apple-cake?' thought Eileen.

'Four pieces of apple-cake, please,' ordered Seamus. 'And three mugs of tea.'

'Four mugs of tea!' said the small man quickly. 'And make it hot, strong, and sweet.'

The woman cut the four pieces. The small man snatched the biggest, opened his mouth wide, pushed in the whole piece and swallowed it. Then he picked up a cup of tea and drank it at one gulp.

'Greedy little creature,' muttered Seamus.

But the white pig nibbled his apple-cake and sipped tea from a saucer so daintily that Eileen could have watched him for ever.

The small man was shaking crumbs out of his long beard; the white pig was draining the last drop of tea from his saucer.

'Let's run!' said Seamus to Eileen. 'I don't want to go round the Fair with a pig. People will think we're a show and laugh at us.'

A horseman came riding by. The children slipped behind him. Then dodging round a stall piled with delph, they ran towards the hobby-horses.

The music was starting, the platform was turning. The horses were rising and falling, their eyes gleaming, the stirrups swinging as they glided round.

Seamus gave a jump, and Eileen, forgetting her wonderful boots, jumped with him, so that instead of landing on the edge of the platform, they sat down in the saddles of two empty horses.

They were both out of breath, but they clung to the twisted golden pole which passed down through each horse and kept their seats.

'I'm glad we got away from those two!' exclaimed Seamus. 'What ails you, Eileen?'

She was staring past him. He turned, and there, climbing on to the quickly turning platform, was the small, ragged man, and after him, the white pig!

'Bother!' said Seamus under his breath.

By this time all the hobby-horses had riders, but the small, ragged man trotted along by Seamus, and when the horse plunged down he jumped up behind.

The white pig stood on his hind legs beside Eileen. He looked at her so pleadingly that she had to help him up and he sat in front of her, grunting with pleasure.

Luckily, when the man came to collect the money, he charged only for Seamus and Eileen.

But Seamus didn't enjoy his ride half as much as he expected, for the small man's whiskers blew in his face and he couldn't see anything at all.

'I'm not going up in a swing with them!' he determined, as the roundabout slowed down and the horses came to a stop.

Seamus and Eileen raced across the Green, but when they reached the boat-swings, the small man and the white pig were there beside them.

'We'll never be able to swing high,' thought Seamus crossly, as the small man clambered over the side of the boat and settled himself on the floor with his pig.

But the moment he and Eileen laid hands on the rope, the boat flew through the air.

Up! Up!! Up!!! until they could look all over the Fair.

They were as high as the tops of the trees and the roofs of the houses.

At first Eileen was scared and shut her eyes when they went soaring into the air.

'Hold fast and you can't fall out!' called Seamus.

The small man and the white pig sprawled on the floor and grinned all over their faces. When Eileen saw this she was ashamed of her fear and tugged harder at the rope to show she didn't mind.

The wind was cold and the children's cheeks tingled. The birds flying by flapped their wings and snapped their beaks as the boat swung low, then high again.

Eileen waved her hand to Long Ears so far below, and he waggled his head, for he was too busy eating to answer.

Seamus looked over the Fair Green, wondering what they should do next.

Eileen looked too. Near the fortune-teller and her birds she saw where a man had set up a board with hooks on it.

Piled on the ground beneath were dozens of wooden rings and boys were throwing them at the hooks.

The man's voice floated up to them as they swung above the crowd.

'Three tries a penny! Three shots out of three and you win a gorgeous prize! A walking-stick, made entirely and completely of clove rock! Three tries a penny! Three tries a penny!'

Eileen could see the clove walking- stick. It was striped in dark brown and light brown, and had a curly handle.

'If I had that I could give every boy and girl in the school a great lump,' she told herself.

'Seamus!' she called. 'Look at the grand walking-stick! I must have three tries!'

Seamus laughed.

'You'd never win it!' he called back. 'Half the boys at the Fair have been trying all day and nobody has won it yet.'

'I'm going to try!' declared Eileen.

'You'll only waste your money,' Seamus told her.

'Time's up!' shouted the man who looked after the swings.

They stopped pulling the ropes and the boat began to go to sleep.

Seamus wondered what the man would say when he saw the four of them, for more than two were forbidden to go on one boat!

Just as the swing slowed down the man looked over his shoulder.

Out jumped the small man and his pig, and away scampered the two of them!

'Good riddance!' said Seamus.

He and Eileen made straight for the board with the hooks and the clove walking-stick.

'Better let me try,' suggested Seamus. 'If I win I'll give you half. Only, I want the handle end.'

Seamus was the better shot, so Eileen was quite willing.

He paid a penny. The man gave him three rings, showed him where to stand and stood back, watching.

'One!'

Seamus threw too high and the ring tapped the board right above the hooks.

'Two!'

He swung round and flung the ring very carefully, but it struck the board too far to the left.

'Three!'

Seamus stood on tiptoe and tossed the ring, but he aimed too high and it went over the top of the board!

'Now I'll try,' said Eileen, pulling out a penny.

'Don't be silly!' exclaimed Seamus. 'You know you can't throw as well as I can.'

'I might be lucky,' protested Eileen. 'And that's a stick worth trying for.'

Seamus knew that Eileen was often very lucky, so he gave in.

Eileen held out her penny. The man gave her three rings.

Eileen looked at the hooks. There were three rows of them: five in each row.

'I'll aim at the middle one,' she decided.

She raised her arm. Just as she let go, someone jogged her elbow.

'That is mean,' she thought, believing Seamus had knocked her for fun.

The ring flew high, curved, came down, and caught on the middle hook. Seamus clapped her on the back. The people standing around drew nearer.

'That's a fine shot!' declared a man who had won a prize at the rifle-range.

Eileen took her second ring.

'Don't joggle me this time!' she whispered to Seamus.

He looked puzzled, but did not speak.

Eileen raised her arm. As she let the ring leave her hand her elbow was tipped.

'Seamus is tiresome!' she said to herself.

The ring sped in a straight line, then dropped suddenly on the centre hook in the top row!

'Hurray!' shouted Seamus, clapping his hands. 'One more, Eileen, and the stick is yours!'

Eileen took the third ring. She felt very nervous.

'You really mustn't jog me this time,' Eileen told Seamus and, as she spoke, she flung the ring.

Yet quickly as she had thrown it, her elbow was knocked.

What did it matter? There was the third ring hanging on the last hook in the bottom row!

'Give her the prize!' shouted Seamus.

'It isn't right!' declared the man who owned the hooks and the rings. 'There was a small chap at the back helping her!'

'She won the three times!' interrupted the man who had been the prize-winner at the rifle range. 'If ye don't give the child her rights I'll have ye run off the Green!'

Still grumbling, the man gave Eileen the huge walking-stick. It was so big she could not carry it by herself and Seamus had to help her.

How the people crowded round as they marched across the Fair Green to the station!

When Long Ears saw them coming with that big stick he was so surprised he raised his ears up straight.

Then he let them drop again, for he knew that a stick with Eileen and Seamus wasn't the same as a stick would be with the tinkers.

'You shall have a piece when we break it up,' Eileen told the little grey donkey as she helped Seamus fix the stick in the cart so that it would be safe.

They started home. Some of the stalls had candles fixed all along the edges, others had tin oil-lamps hung up at the back. The roundabout was a blaze of coloured lights, and the man from whom Eileen had won the clove stick was fixing up a naphtha flare as they passed.

Neither Eileen nor Seamus wanted to leave the Fair and yet they wanted to be home. It was a long, dark road and they were tired.

'It'll be desperate late before we're home,' sighed Seamus.

'Wouldn't you love to be sitting by the fire, telling our adventures?' asked Eileen.

Seamus did not reply. He sprang to his feet and peered into the darkness.

Beside Long Ears trotted a small, ragged man and a white pig. In his hand the small man carried a switch. He tapped Long Ears with it – once! twice! thrice!

'Ah, you're the one who helped Eileen to win!' said Seamus to himself. 'What are you up to now? I wonder.'

The cart gave a jolt. Seamus jumped right out of his seat and back again, with such a bump!

'Isn't it misty on the bridge tonight!' murmured Eileen drowsily.

Seamus stared around him. Was he asleep? Or had he been asleep and just woke up?

Already they had crossed the bridge. Yet it seemed but a few moments before and they were still within hearing of the Fair.

He looked over his shoulder. The moon was rising over the flat-topped mountain and the road was deserted.

He looked ahead – there were the lights of home shining through the mist and darkness.

He looked at Eileen. Her head was nodding and she was half-asleep.

'Maybe it did happen and maybe it didn't,' said Seamus, 'But we're safe home and the journey's ended.'

8

The wrong side of the bed

hat a cold morning it was!

Eileen opened one eye and put the tip of her nose outside the bedclothes to see what was happening. Then without waiting to find out she cuddled down as far as she could under the sheet, the blanket, and the patchwork quilt.

Eileen was dreaming she was with Aunt Una, and Old Andy, and Blackie and Sausage, when she heard Seamus calling her.

'Eileen! Eileen!' he shouted at the top of his voice.

'Wish I needn't get up until summer comes, but I am glad it's a holiday,' thought Eileen drowsily.

Now Seamus was tapping at the little window opposite her bed.

'Eileen! Eileen! Wake up, sleepyhead! There's snow on the ground!'

'Snow!' exclaimed Eileen.

She wriggled a little higher on her pillow, opened her eyes as wide as she could, and sat up in bed.

Seamus was right!

The turf pile, the donkey's stable, the wall, the bushes were all glittering white. The flat-topped mountain, which sometimes looked purple and sometimes black, was white too. And a few big flakes fluttered slowly down from the sky.

Eileen was wide awake now. She was in such a hurry to run out into the snow that instead of jumping on to the strip of carpet which lay across the floor right up to the door just as she did every morning, she slipped out of the wrong side of the bed!

She was still looking through the window, but the moment her bare feet touched the floor she knew what she had done.

'Oo!' she cried. 'Oo! It is cold! Why couldn't Seamus leave me to wake up by myself!'

Eileen felt cross as she dressed. She felt crosser when she came into the kitchen and found the door wide open so that the bitter wind blew in.

'Don't stand there shivering,' said her mother. 'Stack the turf against the wall – there's the girl.'

The turf-cutter was taking sods from the back of the turf pile and throwing them to Seamus, who ran with them into the kitchen.

'Hurry up, Eileen!' said Seamus. 'When we've finished we'll have a snow-fight.'

Eileen had always loved putting the hard black sods against the wall so that there was one less in each row, and if she could end with one sod at the top she was very proud.

It was fun, too, sweeping the broken pieces into a neat heap at the side of the hearth, where they were handy for coaxing up the fire when it died down.

But this morning her fingers were so cold that she kept dropping the sods, and arranged them so carelessly that just as she finished they toppled over and lay scattered about the floor.

'The poor child's freezing,' said her mother. 'Shut the door, Seamus. You've brought in enough turf until after breakfast.'

Seamus came in, warm and glowing, his arms filled with the last load of turf.

'Let me do it,' he said, dropping to his knees.

He wanted to help Eileen, but she was in his way and he gave her a push – only a tiny one!

Eileen was bending, and over she went!

She knocked into Big Fella, the dog, who was sniffing round the table, wondering would breakfast ever be ready.

Big Fella sprang back and one of his big paws went into the cat's saucer of milk.

Rose was a dainty cat, and when the milk splashed over her fur, up went her back, her tail swelled, her whiskers bristled, and she gave Big Fella a scratch to teach him to be more careful.

'Seamus pushed me on purpose,' sobbed Eileen, sitting on the floor.

Big Fella ran howling under the table, Rose leaped on top of the press and crouched there growling, while Seamus squatted back on his heels, wondering what he had done.

The children's mother was putting the porridge in four basins, two big white ones for herself and the turf-cutter, and two small blue ones for Eileen and Seamus.

She started round, thinking something dreadful had happened, and tipped over one of the bowls. The thick porridge ran over the table and trickled down the side.

The kitchen was in a state!

The turf-cutter, hearing the noise, came running across the yard and flung open the door.

He picked Eileen up and gave Seamus a hand to help himself.

'What in the wide world's wrong, girleen?' he asked.

'Seamus pushed me over!' sobbed Eileen. 'It's all his fault!'

'I didn't!' contradicted Seamus. 'Eileen's a horrid little cross-patch.'

'I wonder now,' said their mother, 'did Eileen get out of the wrong side of the bed this morning?'

And, of course, that was just what Eileen had done!

By the time they finished breakfast Eileen began to feel less cross. Seamus was in a hurry to get out in the snow, so he gobbled his porridge without hardly talking at all, Rose came down from the top of the press and had a fresh saucer of milk, Big Fella licked out all the basins and settled down to clearing up the great iron pot.

'Come along, Eileen,' said Seamus. 'Let's have our snow-fight now. I'll go to the back of Long Ears' shed and you can keep in the front.'

He ran off to make snowballs. Eileen stayed behind to lace her boots, and she was so long that Seamus had made two piles of snowballs and still she did not come.

'I'll make her jump when she does come,' chuckled Seamus to himself.

He climbed on top of the donkey's stable, and, as Eileen came peering round it to find out where he was, Seamus pushed a huge slab of snow down on top of her.

Eileen's coat collar was turned up and her tammy pulled down, so that only the smallest bit of snow went inside. But her head and shoulders were covered and she looked so surprised that Seamus laughed and laughed until he almost fell off the shed.

'You do make a fine snow man, Eileen,' he said at last.

Any other day Eileen would have laughed too, and caught up a handful of snow to pelt him. But now she felt so angry that she picked up a sod of turf he had left lying on the path, and flung it straight at his laughing face.

Seamus dodged as he saw it coming and the sod flew right over his head, but Eileen did not wait to see.

As the sod left her hand she was suddenly ashamed and frightened too.

Feeling sure she had hurt Seamus terribly, she ran down the path, through the gate and out on to the road.

'I've been bold ever since I got up, and now I've hurt Seamus real bad and he'll never forgive me. I'll run away and join the gipsies!' said Eileen.

9
Aboard the barge

O n ran Eileen until she was out of breath. She shook off the snow Seamus had thrown over her, but the air was now filled with dancing flakes. They clung to her coat, her tammy, her eyelashes, and when she reached the bridge and leaned on the rail at the side, she saw them falling into the dark water.

She saw something else!

Just under the bank, where he had found a nice, comfortable hole, was the water-rat. There he sat combing his whiskers and looking up at Eileen with his sharp bright eyes.

'Isn't this Eileen?' he seemed to be asking. 'But where is Seamus? And what has become of Long Ears?'

Eileen bent down to talk to him.

'I'm running away!' she explained. 'I'm never going home any more!'

The water-rat was so shocked to hear this, that he turned his back on Eileen and, with a quiver of his tail, scuttled into his hole, while Eileen felt so unhappy that she began to cry, and her big tears washed away the snow-flakes clinging to her eyelashes.

She walked on beside the canal. She knew the gipsies had gone that way, for only yesterday she and Seamus had seen their bright green caravan with the tiny windows and the steps at the back.

The roof of the van was piled high with wicker tables and chairs, and a fat, red-faced woman drove the grey horse.

'If I walk quickly I shall soon find them,' thought Eileen. 'Gipsies never travel far.'

But the snow was falling so thickly that she could scarcely see where she was going and she had to lift her feet at every step.

It was so cold and there was not a sound to be heard. Eileen talked to herself for company.

'I wish I could see the roadman's fire,' she said. 'But I wouldn't like him to see me. That wouldn't do at all!'

Eileen was sure she had reached the place where the roadman ought to be. She could feel the big rough stones which he spread over the road to fill up the holes, but there wasn't a sign of him, or his queer little shelter, or the fire he made in a pail to keep himself warm.

Suddenly she saw quite close to the path something big and dark. There was the hot, pleasant smell of coffee, and someone was whistling *The Top of Cork Road*.

'That's Tim Quinlan!' said Eileen. 'But where is he?'

She rubbed the snow from her eyes. There was the turf-barge she and Seamus and her father and mother had journeyed in all the way to Dublin, and close up beside it was the roadman's shelter and his glowing pail!

She couldn't see Tim Quinlan because he was inside his shelter. She couldn't see the captain of the barge either, but she could hear him talking away.

'Captain Cassidy!' called Eileen.

The snow muffled her voice and he did not hear her.

In a moment Eileen was glad of this, for she was ashamed to let the captain or Tim Quinlan know she had hurt Seamus and run away.

The barge was moored close to the bank, and Eileen, holding fast to the thick tarred rope which fastened it to a tree, stepped on board.

Between two piles of turf was a narrow passage, and when Eileen entered this she was sheltered from the snow.

On tiptoe she walked along until, just peeping round she found herself right behind Captain Cassidy.

His legs were stretched out towards Tim Quinlan's fire, and they both looked so comfortable that Eileen felt colder and more miserable than before.

Tim was the best whistler in the whole of Munster, and he was a great friend of Eileen's; but just now she was far more interested in Captain Cassidy.

He was drinking coffee from a big tin billy-can, and on a box beside him were half a loaf of brown crusty bread and a huge piece of cheese.

He took a long drink and wiped his mouth with the end of his long beard. Then with his clasp-knife he cut off a lump of bread and a smaller piece of cheese and crammed them into his mouth.

Eileen felt that it was hours and hours since breakfast. If only she had waited until after dinner to run away!

'There's eating and drinking in coffee,' said Captain Cassidy, with his mouth full.

Tim Quinlan did not answer. He was whistling the first bar of *Barney O'Hea*, and when Tim started on a tune it didn't matter what happened, he kept on until he had finished.

'I wonder will the snow be stopping soon,' said Captain Cassidy.

Tim hadn't finished his tune, so there was no answer to that. Captain Cassidy had another drink of coffee and another bite of bread and cheese.

'I don't remember such troublesome weather for generations,' said the captain when his mouth was almost empty.

But Tim was now in the middle of *The Rakes of Mallow*.

Captain Cassidy sighed and went on eating.

At last he only half-filled his mouth, so that he finished eating and Tim stopped whistling at the same time.

'Did ye see which way them gipsies went, Tim?' asked the captain quickly before Tim could start another tune.

Eileen was almost as anxious as Captain Cassidy to hear Tim speak. She leaned so far forward that she nearly tumbled over, and to save herself put down her hand right on top of the bread and cheese.

But Tim did not speak. He just shook his head and was whistling again as Eileen drew back without being discovered.

In her hand she held all that was left of the captain's lunch.

He took one more drink from the billy-can. Then, without looking round, reached for his bread and cheese. His fingers groped over the top of the box without finding any. He looked over his shoulder frowning and, pushing back his battered old caubeen, scratched his head.

'I could 'a' sworn there was another bite left,' he muttered.

In searching for his bread and cheese he had shifted the billy-can so that it was out of sight. The coffee was still hot and the fragrant steam rose up in Eileen's face.

'There's only a tiny drop left,' she thought. 'He'll never mind that.'

And, snatching up the can, she drank all the captain had left.

Captain Cassidy tilted his seat back and drew the can towards him. He lifted it to his lips, took it away, stared inside, then put it down and glared across at Tim Quinlan.

'See here, me lad,' he said; 'that's not a nice joke to be playin' on a man!'

Tim was halfway through the first part of *The Blackbird*. He had to finish, and while Captain Cassidy waited he got angrier and angrier.

At last Tim spoke.

'What ails ye, man?' he asked.

'What ails me?' repeated the captain. 'Is that what ye're askin', Tim Quinlan? Ye steal me bread and cheese on me, ye drink me coffee and then ye ask – what ails me?'

'Have sense, captain!' exclaimed Tim. 'Amn't I sittin' here before ye, an' how could I touch yer food an' drink an' you not knowin'? 'Tis dreamin' ye are.'

And he began whistling again.

Captain Cassidy shook his fist in Tim Quinlan's face.

'Will ye stop that rediculous noise, an' not be tormentin' me! There's us two alone here, an' my food an' drink have been stolen on me. I want to know the reason why.'

Tim Quinlan leaped across his fire and pulled the captain's beard.

'Call me a thief an' a robber, will ye?' he demanded wrathfully. 'It's sorry I am that ever I brought meself an' me belongin's near yer old turf-barge.'

Captain Cassidy tugged his beard out of Tim's grasp and, catching up his billy-can, hurled it in the roadman's face.

Terrified at what she had done, Eileen, for the second time that day, ran away.

As she hurried along the barge she caught her foot on a rope and went sprawling. A pile of turf crashed down and the sound made the two men stop quarrelling.

'It's the thief!' shouted Captain Cassidy. 'After him, Tim!'

Eileen jumped up, sprang to the shore, and sped down the road as fast as she could.

The captain and Tim Quinlan did not follow her far. In a few yards she was out of sight and she could hear them talking as they returned to the fire.

'I'll go back home,' said Eileen to herself. 'I keep on doing bad things. But even if Seamus is angry with me all day, he'll forgive me tomorrow. Sure he will! I'll tell him I never meant to hurt him!'

The thought of being once more with her mother and father and Seamus in the cosy cabin by the bog made her almost happy again.

Then she discovered that she was still holding the captain's bread and cheese. She was about to fling it away when she felt terribly hungry. Perhaps she ought to take it back. But she was so tired. She broke off a tiny piece of crust and nibbled it. Then she took a bite of cheese, and after that she didn't stop until she had eaten every morsel.

On she trudged. What a long way it was to the bridge!

'I wish I'd never thought of running away,' sighed Eileen.

She did not guess that in her haste and confusion she had turned the wrong way, and every moment she was

going farther and farther from home.

10

A strange guide

ileen was so sleepy from the cold that her eyes began to close as she walked along. Suddenly she opened them wide and shook her head in amazement.

'I don't remember this place at all,' she said to herself.

Without noticing, she had entered a wood. The ground was dry underfoot and the spreading trees kept out the snow, so that only a few flakes drifted down between the branches, looking as if they too were lost.

Now that there was no snow to blind her Eileen could see about her quite easily, though the light was dim and grey. The trees stood in rows, as if they were drilling, and high up, Eileen saw the snow lying on the topmost branches.

She sat down on a fallen trunk to rest. A fat little robin, with a red breast and browny-grey wings, hopped close up to her with his head on one side.

'Weet-a-weet!' said the robin in a friendly voice.

'I haven't even a crumb to give you,' Eileen told him sadly.

The robin hopped away. When he had gone a little way he stopped and looked back. He gave a few more hops – then looked back again.

'Do you want me to come with you?' asked Eileen.

She stood up and went softly forward. On went the robin, hop, hop!

Now that Eileen was following he went quickly, fluttering in and out among the trees. Then waiting.

The trees grew closer together, the branches overhead were thicker, and it was so dark that Eileen lost sight of her little guide.

She stared around in terror. Ah! There he was!

Eileen ran towards a red patch she saw right ahead.

'That's not the robin!' she exclaimed in disappointment 'It's a fire!'

The red light glowed on the tree-trunks, on the leaf-strewn ground, and on the bare branches rising up into the air.

Eileen danced with excitement.

'I must have got back to the barge!' she cried, wondering how it could have happened.

As she spoke she discovered that she was coming to a grassy glade. The trees stood away from it, and the snow was falling down and drifting up against the wheels of a bright green caravan drawn back against a high pile of logs.

How warm and snug the red glow looked as it streamed out through the white muslin curtains!

The robin was perched on the steps at the back. As Eileen ran out from the shelter of the trees he gave a satisfied little 'twee-tweet!' and flew away.

'Will the gipsies be kind to me?' wondered Eileen, feeling very small and timid.

She stood at the foot of the steps looking up at the door. It had a brass handle and a twisted knocker, just like the door to a house in the street of a town. Eileen lifted her hand to raise the knocker when she heard a harsh voice singing:

> 'Clean the windows, shut the door;
> Shine the knives and wash the floor;
> Shake the mat and black the grate;
> Never mind the babies – they can wait.
> Sweep the hearth, then scrub! scrub! scrub!
> Rub-a-dub! Oh, rub-a-dub!'

'That's the strangest gipsy song I ever heard,' said Eileen to herself.

She crept to the nearest window and, by standing on tiptoe, managed to see into the caravan.

It was the cleanest, tidiest place Eileen had ever set eyes on.

There was a black, shiny range at the end opposite the door, and it was from this the glow came. On top was a round saucepan with two handles and a copper kettle. They both gleamed as if they had been polished only that moment.

At one side of the stove there were shelves with cups, saucers, and plates neatly arranged.

At the other side was a box, covered with clean newspaper. On it was a frying-pan which was so bright you could have used it as a looking-glass. Inside the box were three iron pots fitted inside one another.

Between the windows hung gay pictures and calendars. The mantelpiece was crowded with brass ornaments.

Eileen saw a little man carrying a spade and a bucket, a dog with a curly tail, a horse, a tiny armchair, an elephant, with its trunk raised aloft and a seat on its back, and all these were made of shining brass.

'What lovely toys!' gasped Eileen. 'But I don't think I want to live in there!'

In the middle of the van was a wooden table, and at it stood the fat, red-faced woman Eileen had seen driving the caravan the day before.

She wore a green frock with the sleeves rolled up, a white apron fastened round her waist, and her head was tied up in a duster.

She was polishing a pile of forks and spoons, and as she rubbed she sang her song.

If a cinder dropped on the hearth she rushed to pick it up with the tongs; then she took out a handbroom and a dust-pan and swept up the hearth. She kept on looking round and, snatching a duster which lay ready on the table, she would dart at a picture, set it straight, dust it, wipe the glass, then back to her polishing.

Eileen heard another sound beside the singing. At first she couldn't make out what it was at all. But at last, by stretching her neck as much as she possibly could, she saw a queer-looking box in a corner. It was covered with a stiff, white, frilly cloth, and, sticking up their funny round heads out of it, were two babies.

Their mouths were wide open and they were screaming, but the gipsy woman sang and polished, and never took any notice of them.

'I'm sure she must be wanting someone to mind the babies,' thought Eileen, stepping away from the window.

Then she saw the grey horse!

He was tethered to a tree. A rug was thrown over him, there was hay spread thickly on the ground and his nose-bag was full, but he was the most mournful-looking horse Eileen had met.

'If I knew the way home I'd get on your back and ride

there,' said Eileen to the grey horse.

11

Minding the babies

s Eileen spoke she put her hand on the rope which fastened the grey horse. To her surprise it lifted up its head and neighed so loudly that she jumped away and stood trembling.

It was such a noise that the trees around shook and the snow fell from their branches, while the door of the green caravan was flung open and down the steps rushed the gipsy woman.

'Who's that trying to steal my grey horse?' she shouted, staring about her.

Eileen kept so quiet that the woman didn't see her, but at last she caught sight of the red tammy.

'Here's the thief!' she cried in triumph, leaping at Eileen and catching hold of her by the arm.

'Please, ma'am, I wasn't stealing your grey horse. Do let me go!' pleaded Eileen, for the angry gipsy was pinching her arm and shaking her until she seemed to be falling to pieces.

'You weren't stealing my horse, weren't you? Then what were you doing?' demanded the woman.

'I – I was just coming to ask if you wanted anyone to

mind the babies,' stammered Eileen.

'Well, come and mind them,' said the gipsy, and she marched Eileen up the steps, pushed her into the caravan, and shut the door.

The babies stopped screaming to blink up at Eileen, but soon they started again. The noise made Eileen's head ache, but it was grand to be in there with the warm stove!

'It's a terrible cold day, ma'am,' she said politely.

'Feed the babies!' commanded the gipsy woman. 'Take down those dishes!' She pointed towards the shelves by the stove. 'Fill them with gruel!' and she pointed to the big round saucepan.

Eileen took down the dishes. There was a big, iron spoon hanging at the back of the stove, and with this she ladled out the gruel.

Eileen got a small spoon and, dipping it into one of the dishes, took up a little.

How good it smelt! But the gipsy woman looked so cross as she polished her forks and spoons and sang her song that Eileen dared not ask for any.

> 'All day long I scrub and sweep,
> While the babies scream and weep.
> All day long I clean and shine.
> What a busy life is mine!
> Shine and clean, sweep and scrub.
> Rub-a-dub! Oh, rub-a-dub!'

'I don't like that song at all,' Eileen thought to herself. As soon as the gruel was cool enough, she put the spoon to the nearest baby's mouth.

It gulped the spoonful down and opened its mouth again.

'You'll have to take turns,' Eileen told the babies.

'That's the fairest way.'

She was about to give a spoonful to the second baby when the woman thumped the table.

'Where's the other spoon?' she asked angrily. 'You can't feed two babies with one spoon!'

'Maybe I'd better finish with one at the time?' suggested Eileen.

'You'd better not, me fine madam!' replied the gipsy.

So Eileen fed the babies in turn, each with its own spoon, from its own dish. While one ate the other screamed, until poor Eileen was so confused that she began to mix the spoons up.

The gipsy woman was watching her and, leaning across the table, boxed her ears.

'Cheating me poor little children, are you!' she exclaimed. 'A fine job I've in front of me! I don't know what girls are coming to, indeed I don't! But you'll have a chance to learn when the rest of the caravans come.'

'Will I have to mind more babies?' asked Eileen.

'There's twenty, all told,' replied the gipsy. 'But there isn't one of them as good and sweet as mine,' she added proudly.

She had to shout, for the babies were making a terrible uproar because Eileen had stopped feeding them. She quickly began spooning out the gruel again.

'If Seamus saw me now, he'd be real sorry for me. I know he would,' thought Eileen. 'These must be the noisiest, greediest babies in the world. Oh, if only I could get back home again!'

And her tears fell into the gruel.

Suddenly the grey horse neighed. The sound made Eileen start, and she dropped a spoonful of gruel on the spotless, white table.

'Just wait till I come back! You dirty, untidy girl!' stormed the gipsy, as she dashed out of the caravan.

She was in such a hurry that she forgot to shut the door after her.

Eileen, taking no notice of the babies, slipped through the door, and, thinking only of escaping from the gipsy, ran noiselessly across the snow and plunged into the darkness of the wood.

She heard the grey horse neighing, the gipsy woman shouting; but she had found a path and, going more slowly, she managed to follow it until she was out of hearing.

'This must lead somewhere,' she was thinking hopefully, when she heard the rattle of tins, shouting and laughing, and a great many people talking all at once.

'Now I can find out the way home!' exclaimed Eileen joyfully, and she began to run towards the sounds.

At once she crashed into a bush. The sounds she had heard stopped suddenly, and the wood was as silent as if Eileen were the only person in it.

A light flickered and danced among the trees. It made them look strange and frightening. Some were like serpents coiled to spring, others like bears standing on their hind legs, others crouched like lions.

Eileen hid behind a tree and peered out.

'They're only trees,' she told herself. 'It's the light makes them so queer!'

'Halt! Who goes there?' called a voice.

'It's only me – Eileen, and I'm not moving an inch,' she answered in a trembling voice.

The light came nearer. The trees stopped looking strange and terrifying, and Eileen saw a torch, flaring and smoking, held up by a tall man with a yellow handkerchief

bound round his head.
He was the Tinker Chief !

12

The Tinker Chief

he light from the torch made the Tinker Chief's shadow run ahead of him. It crouched so that it was like a dwarf hunched up on the ground, then stretched up until its head was lost in the high branches of the trees.

Eileen would have been afraid of the shadow if she had seen it before she knew who was carrying the torch. But she felt quite sure the dark man wouldn't hurt her.

She ran along the path to him.

'Please take me home!' she said.

The Tinker Chief looked down at her.

'If it isn't the girleen that stole me donkey on me!' he exclaimed.

Eileen stamped her foot.

'I haven't stolen anything!' she cried out in anger. 'The captain called me a thief, the gipsy woman said I wanted to steal her grey horse, and you say I stole Long Ears. All I've taken was just a bite of the captain's bread and cheese and a small, wee sup of his coffee, and I think it's horrid and mean of everybody!'

As soon as the last word was out of her mouth Eileen

85

wished she hadn't spoken.

'What will he do to me?' she thought in terror.

But the Tinker Chief wasn't angry at all. He flung back his head and laughed and laughed until all the other tinkers came rushing through the wood to find out what fun they were missing.

'Ho, ho! Just look at her!' he shouted. 'She's the size of me thumb an' she's the pluck of a giant. Come along to our camp, me ragin' cock sparrer! I'm thinkin' we'd better make a tinker of ye!'

Eileen put her hand in his and they went through the wood, the whole army of tinkers bundling after them, until she saw the camp.

A great bonfire blazed in the centre of a stony hollow. On it a huge cauldron sent out a delightful smell and on the ground around were scattered basins, cups without handles, empty tin cans, cracked plates, enamel plates with the enamel chipped off, lids of saucepans, battered spoons.

An old woman, with a hump on her back and a tattered shawl drawn over her head, stirred the cauldron with a huge iron spoon.

As the Tinker Chief came up to the fire with Eileen and flung down his torch, crushing the flame out under his heel, the old woman left off stirring and pointed at Eileen with the iron spoon.

'What stranger is this ye're bringing to our fire?' she asked.

'A friend. Feed her well!' answered the dark man sharply.

He sat on a heap of sacks and pulled Eileen down beside him. The old woman, muttering to herself, began to spoon out what was cooking in the cauldron. She served first the Tinker Chief, then Eileen with a tin can so full that the thick soup trickled over the sides.

Eileen took a rusty spoon from the ground and dipped it into her soup. There were pieces of meat chopped up in it, carrots, turnips, onions, crusts of bread. Every spoonful brought up something different.

'This is the best food I have ever eaten,' thought Eileen, as she scraped the tin clean.

'Now we'll hear what brings you alone in our wood,' said the Tinker Chief.

The tinkers who had finished eating turned towards Eileen. Those who hadn't, hurried so that they could listen properly. Eileen was shy, with all those bright eyes watching her; but she knew there was no chance of getting home until she had told her story, so she began at once.

When she sang the gipsy song, they rocked backwards and forwards with laughter.

'Is that a story worth telling?' asked the chief, looking round on his people.

'It is, indeed!' they shouted.

'Listen, now!' he said to Eileen. 'When you go back to your own people, you'll tell them how much better than the gipsies the tinkers are.'

'Indeed, I will,' promised Eileen.

'There's some praise the gipsies for making brushes and chairs and telling the future, but isn't a fine tin saucepan or a frying-pan more use?' he asked.

'Indeed, yes,' replied Eileen, though she couldn't see signs of anything at all made by the tinkers.

'And if we do take a few miserable cabbages, or an odd fowl or rabbit, haven't we mouths to fill, and don't we share with them that needs it?'

'You do, indeed,' Eileen told him. 'And I'll tell every one how good you've been to me.'

'Maybe the girleen doesn't want to go back,' said the old woman who had stirred the cauldron. 'She's grand and comfortable here with us, and she can tell a fine story and sing a grand song. Aren't we often dull an' lonesome without anyone who can tell of strange doings?'

While the old woman was speaking, a thin girl with a mop of black hair crept up behind Eileen and snatched away her red tammy. Eileen pretended not to know. She feared the tinkers would not let her go, that they would take her boots and her coat away and that she would never see her mother or her father or Seamus again!

Eileen looked sadly at the dark man. He stared straight into the fire and sat so still that she thought he must have forgotten all about her.

'You said I was your friend, and I was sure you'd take me home,' she whispered.

'And I will!' he shouted, springing to his feet so suddenly that the old woman tumbled over and the other tinkers cried out in alarm.

Eileen jumped up. She was just as eager to escape from the tinkers as she had been to get away from the gipsy caravan.

The Tinker Chief plunged his torch into the fire and relighted it. Swinging round, he saw the red tammy on the tinker girl's head and, grabbing it away, handed it to Eileen.

'Put your best foot foremost,' he told Eileen, and strode away from the camp.

Eileen had to run to keep up with him. Her feet were sore, her knees trembled, her head ached. She stumbled along, determined not to be left behind. But as they came out of the wood on to the road, she fell down in the snow.

The Tinker Chief looked back. Eileen did not get up. She was too tired. The snow was soft and she shut her eyes.

She felt him lifting her.

'What ye're needin' is a flyin' angel,' he said.

There she was – up on his shoulder, and he marching along with the torch, sending out a stream of sparks and smoke, which flew behind them like a banner.

It was wonderful to sit there, looking down along the dark road. But who was that calling her: 'Eileen! Eileen!'

'I must be asleep and dreaming,' she thought, for the voices came along the canal, over the bog, down from the hills, and across the winding road.

'Did ye hear that?' asked the tinker, looking sideways at her; so she knew she wasn't asleep at all, but wide awake.

'They're looking for me,' said Eileen. 'Oh, I do want to be home again!'

'She's here – safe and sound!' roared the tinker. But the wind carried his voice away, and still they could hear 'Eileen! Eileen!' called from north and south and east and west.

'Hold tight on to me!' commanded the dark man, and he set off running so that Eileen had to cling fast to his head to keep her seat on his shoulder.

There was the barge and the roadman's shelter, but the captain and Tim Quinlan were no longer there. They were away searching on the other bank of the canal.

The tinker did not stop. He ran with long steady strides which took them along at a great rate, and there they were at the bridge.

He stopped and set Eileen down.

'May you never lack fire or food,' he said, and before she could say 'Thank you,' or 'Good-bye,' he was racing in the direction of the wood.

'Eileen! Eileen!' called the voices.

'I'm here!' answered Eileen. She spoke so faintly that she scarcely heard it herself, but the wind bore her words in the right direction and Long Ears knew her voice.

'Hee-haw!' he sang out, and Eileen knew she was found.

A light came swinging along the tow-path. That belonged to Tim Quinlan. A faint glimmer floated down from the hills. That was Seamus, holding a candle and riding Long Ears. The storm lantern the turf-cutter used danced across the bog like a will-o'-the-wisp, and the big steady glow of a kitchen lamp advanced on the road and Eileen knew her mother carried it.

All the lights came together at the crossroads. But Long Ears refused to stay there.

'Hee-haw!' he called. 'Hee-haw!' and in spite of all Seamus could do, he came clattering on to the bridge.

'Seamus!' cried Eileen, catching him by the coat. 'Seamus!'

She couldn't be quite sure, but she thought she saw tears in his eyes, as he jumped off Long Ears's back and hugged her.

'Eileen's on the bridge!' he shouted, and all the lights hurried together so that there was a great blaze, which the tinkers saw from the shelter of the wood, as the turf-cutter and his wife, the captain and Tim Quinlan came running on to the bridge.

Eileen had never been made such a fuss of before.

'The poor child!' sighed her mother, putting her arms round her.

'I never want to know a worse day!' exclaimed the turf-cutter, stroking her face.

The captain and Tim Quinlan patted her on the back and said how splendid it was to have her safe before the long, cold night was really on them.

'But what happened to you?' asked Seamus suddenly as they went towards the cabin. 'I saw you running down the garden after I pushed the snow on top of you and when I jumped off the stable you were gone.'

Eileen's face grew nearly as red as her tammy. She was sitting behind her brother, and she hid her eyes on his shoulder so that she wouldn't see anyone frowning.

'I ran away to join the gipsies!' she said, feeling horribly ashamed of herself.

'Ran away?' they all cried out.

Eileen nodded.

'I thought I'd hurt Seamus when I threw the sod of turf at him. So I ran away!'

'Oh, Eileen!' sighed her mother, looking at her reproachfully. 'How could you?'

'It was my fault!' declared Seamus. 'I shouldn't have teased her.'

'Sure, she'll never do it again when she knows how bad we felt it,' the turf-cutter said, nodding his head firmly.

'Wasn't she the foolish girsha!' exclaimed the captain, looking at Tim Quinlan severely.

But the roadman was whistling *The Low-backed Car* and couldn't stop to talk about anything.

'I'll never run away again, whatever happens, as long as I live!' promised Eileen, and Long Ears had to stand still while they hugged her again.

The cabin door was wide open. When Eileen saw the glowing fire on the hearth, the shining blue-and-white delph on the dresser, and the table laid for the dinner no one had eaten, she was so glad she could hardly speak.

They had dinner and tea all at once, and the captain and Tim Quinlan stayed to help them eat it. Eileen told her adventures. When the captain heard who had taken his bread and cheese he looked at Tim Quinlan and Tim Quinlan looked at him. Then they both had a good look at Eileen, as though they had never seen her before.

'Who would have thought it, now!' exclaimed Tim, and that was the only scolding, and you couldn't call it that, which Eileen received.

The turf-cutter told one of his best stories, the captain related how he had been shipwrecked, Tim Quinlan whistled his gayest tunes, so that one way and another, they had a grand time of it.

But Eileen has made one very important resolution – she is never, never again, going to get out of bed on the wrong side!

13

Four-leaf shamrocks

ileen and Seamus had gathered a basketful of shamrock for their uncle in America. They picked out the best sprays and packed them in moss. The rest they put in water to keep until St. Patrick's Day.

Each morning it seemed fresher and greener than the day before, and one thing was certain – no one would be wearing a finer bunch on the great morning!

'I wish I could find a four-leaf shamrock,' said Eileen as she poured a cup of fresh water into the bowl.

Seamus cocked his nose in the air.

'You're always wanting something!' he declared. 'And if you did find a four-leaf shamrock, what would you do with it?'

'If you hold a four-leaf shamrock in your left hand at dawn on St. Patrick's Day you get what you want very much but haven't wished for.'

'That is silly!' exclaimed Seamus laughing. 'Who told you that?'

'Aunt Una, the time we stayed with her. You'd believe Aunt Una, wouldn't you?' asked Eileen.

Seamus nodded. He thought quite as much of Aunt

Una, who was young and pretty, and jolly, as Eileen did. And he felt it would be grand to find a four-leaf shamrock, but he wouldn't say so.

When Eileen asked him to come with her to gather primroses, he slung the basket over his arm and set off without a single grumble.

Eileen knew the best place for primroses – on the lower slopes of the flat-topped mountain among the bracken.

Seamus knew the best place for shamrock – and that was along the canal bank towards the woods.

They raced along until they reached the bridge.

Eileen ran across and stood looking down at the water. 'Water-rat! Water-rat!' she called.

But the water-rat was out hunting his dinner and could not hear her.

Eileen went on a little way. Suddenly she stopped. Why was Seamus lagging behind?

'Slow-coach!' she cried, for he was still at the other side of the bridge.

'I'm going this way!' he shouted and began walking along the canal bank.

'I don't believe he wants to get primroses at all!' thought Eileen to herself.

But as Seamus had the basket she ran back across the bridge and caught up to him.

'Why do you want to go this way?' asked Eileen.

Seamus got very red.

'Why shouldn't I find a four-leaf shamrock?' he muttered gruffly.

He didn't want to be laughed at. But Eileen was delighted.

'I'll help you,' she promised. 'And while we're searching, we'll think of what we want most.'

They marched along like soldiers – left, right! left, right!

'Here we are!' exclaimed Seamus. 'This is where we found the best shamrock. You go this way. I'll go that way.'

They put down the basket to mark the place they started from. Picking ordinary shamrock is fun, but hunting for a four-leaf shamrock is hard work, and Eileen soon grew tired of it.

'I wish I hadn't told Seamus what Aunt Una said,' she thought to herself.

Eileen's back ached from stooping; her eyes ached from trying to see a four-leaf shamrock among the three-leaf. She tried kneeling down and wriggling along that way. In next to no time her knees were sore and there were two big holes in her stockings, one on each knee.

At last she gave up searching and sat down.

The sun was shining and they were so near to the woods that the trees sheltered her from the wind. The birds were building their nests and Eileen watched them working away, stopping to sing, then working again.

Some were building in the trees, others were busy among the bushes that were scattered in groups across the common, while one was carrying bits of dried grass, tiny twigs, and even a feather to a hole in the ground.

What a fuss they made, chattering and scolding, fluttering their wings and bragging over every bit of straw or twig they used!

Only one was idle – a robin who flew from tree to tree, watching the others, with his head on one side and his bright little eyes twinkling, as though he were laughing at them all.

'You lazy bird!' Eileen called out. 'When those birds

have grand nests to live in, you'll have to sit out on a branch all by yourself!'

The robin seemed to know she was talking to him. He hopped down on the ground and came near. Suddenly Eileen remembered him. He was the bird who led her to the gipsy caravan when she had run away!

He picked up a seed, held it in his beak, tipped his head back and swallowed it. Twittering gaily he strutted about. What was he saying?

> 'A sunny day – sing and play!
> Clouds and rain – work is vain!
> Winds ablow – come and go!
> How they chatter! Does it matter?'

The robin pounced at another seed which had been lying in a crack all the winter and was beginning to sprout. He looked such a scamp that Eileen had to laugh. She didn't want to scare him away, but she made more noise than she thought, for he spread his wings and shot up into the air!

Eileen watched him until he disappeared behind the trees.

Suddenly she jumped up. High in the air gleamed a silver bird. The whirring of its wings came down to her.

'Look, Seamus!' she cried. 'Look, quick! Oh, the lovely bird!'

She glanced over her shoulder. Seamus, his hand shielding his eyes from the sun, was staring in the opposite direction.

Eileen ran back to him.

'Not that way, Seamus!' she said. 'See, over there!'

Seamus looked at the silver bird scornfully.

'That's not a bird, you little silly! That's an aeroplane. But there over the trees – that is a bird! You'll see it soon. Watch!'

At first Eileen could see nothing, then a dark patch against a cloud, scarcely larger than a robin. A rush of outspread wings, gleaming like gold where they caught the sun, and the giant bird was over their heads!

They heard no sound, but it swept through the air, high above, higher than the aeroplane!

Eileen forgot the little birds just beginning to build their nests in the woods.

'That's a golden eagle,' said Seamus softly. 'I'd give everything I've got to find out where it builds its nest!'

'That would be easy if you were up in the aeroplane,' Eileen told him.

When both the golden eagle and the aeroplane were out of sight the children turned homewards.

They walked silently, Seamus thinking about the golden eagle and Eileen wondering would her mother be very angry because of the holes in her stockings.

The bridge was in sight before they remembered that they were returning empty handed.

'Bother! I've forgotten the four-leaf shamrock!' exclaimed Seamus.

'And we've left the basket behind!' cried Eileen.

They did not want to go back for it, so they stood there, feeling very cross with each other and not knowing why.

Suddenly a laughing voice called their names and, turning, they saw Long Ears trotting up the road, the cart behind him and, sitting in the cart, their mother.

In her hand she held two tiny boxes.

'One each,' she said as they scrambled up beside her.

'Now who could be so foolish as to send us shamrock?' asked Seamus.

But Eileen opened hers.

Inside was a green-and-silver harp, and fastened on the edge was a four-leaf shamrock!

There was one for Seamus too, and it was Aunt Una who had sent them.

You'd think they would have been out of bed long before sunrise on St. Patrick's Day, but they were only out just in time to get to Mass. The queer thing was that though they wore their harps so proudly they had forgotten all that the four-leaf shamrock might have done for them. Indeed, it wasn't until they were coming home again that they thought of anything but the grand time they were having – no lessons, no work – a whole day's holiday in the middle of the week!

They were coming along the main street, walking in the middle of the road because of the crowd, when Seamus stopped so suddenly that his father, who was just behind bumped into him.

'What ails thee lad?' he exclaimed crossly, for he was lighting his pipe and now he had to begin all over again.

'Nothing at all,' replied Seamus and went on again; but Eileen knew he was bothering, for he didn't say a word until they reached Mrs. Murphy's.

'Isn't it silly to be coming this way when I haven't even a farthing!' he grumbled.

The turf-cutter's pipe was sending out a cloud of smoke by this time, and he stood with it in his hand while he felt in his pockets.

'Here's sixpence each,' he said to the children. 'Don't be too long spending it, for there's a grand dinner at home waiting for us. Be waiting with Long Ears in a half-hour.'

Mrs. Murphy kept the best shop in the whole town. She put a bit of everything she had in the window and she was a busy woman, so the front of the shop hadn't much style about it, but inside it would do your heart good to see what she had to sell.

Eileen didn't bother to look in the window.

'I know what I'm going to buy,' she told Seamus, and began to squeeze in.

Seamus stood staring at the window, trying to make up his mind.

He had mounted the step when Eileen came out carefully carrying a toy aeroplane.

'Mrs. Murphy hasn't time to show me how to do it, but I'll soon find out,' she told Seamus.

'That's what I wanted!' declared Seamus. 'You said you wanted a skipping-rope!'

'Maybe she has another aeroplane,' said Eileen. 'If she hasn't I'll let you fly this when I don't want to.'

Seamus reached the counter. He knew that Mrs. Murphy wouldn't have another aeroplane, but hanging on the wall was a huge surprise packet.

'Please give me that!' he shouted at the top of his voice, for every one in the shop was pushing and shouting and asking to be served.

He pointed straight at the surprise packet, but Mrs. Murphy was deaf as well as short-sighted, and she gave him a parcel lying on a shelf.

Seamus was pushed away from the counter, so he took his parcel to the door to examine it.

'A pack of birdseed!' he exclaimed. 'Now what in the wide world could I do with that!'

He was about to push back, when his coat was tugged from behind.

'Give it to me!' said a sharp voice. 'I'm terrible hungry! I'm starving!'

Seamus looked over his shoulder. He was so surprised at what he saw that he tumbled backwards off the step into the roadway.

'How did you get here?' he asked in amazement, for, staring greedily at the bag of birdseed, was the golden eagle he had seen flying high in the air when he was searching for a four-leaf shamrock!

The eagle did not answer. It snatched the packet from Seamus, tore it open, scattered the seed over the ground and began gobbling it up.

The eagle's beak was curved and it was very hard for it to pick up the seeds. It looked so comical that Seamus laughed.

The great bird gave Seamus such an angry glare that he jumped up, ready to run away.

'I d-didn't know eagles ate birdseed!' he stammered.

The eagle ate every seed it could find. Then it gave a great sigh.

'Is there anything wrong?' asked Seamus timidly.

The eagle sighed again.

'It's lost I am,' it replied mournfully. 'I'm terrible at finding me way about an' the wind's been choppin' an' changin' an' battin' me from pillar to post till I'm dizzy. How I'm to get a nest built an' eggs laid by Easter divil a wan o' me knows!'

'Maybe I could help you,' suggested Seamus eagerly. 'I'm grand at geography. I'm good at sums an' I'm a fine whistler. If it was stories now, or poetry, you'd have to ask Eileen. But I can tell you anything that's printed on the map – I mean the places printed big!'

The eagle shook its head.

'You'd never be able to tell me – well I know that! It's terrible with Easter comin' so early, an' the other birds gettin' a start on me.'

'Let me try!' urged Seamus.

The eagle rattled its great curved beak.

'I'm huntin' an' searchin' for the Wise Woman of Youghal. She's the wan could tell me where to build me nest an' not have me ashamed before all the little scraps of birds that haven't the courage or the strength to be great travellers.'

'Youghal!' shouted Seamus. 'Of course I can tell you where Youghal is. It's east of Cork!'

'Listen to that now!' exclaimed the eagle. 'Isn't he the clever lad! But where's the use in tellin' me Youghal is east of Cork if I'm not at Cork? An' if you put me down in the middle of Cork itself, how would I know east from west? Tell me that now!'

The eagle sat down on its tail in the dust and sighed deeply.

'Let me get up on your back and let you rise into the air and I'll soon show you the way to Cork,' said Seamus conceitedly.

'Come along, then,' agreed the eagle, going sideways up to Seamus.

Seamus put one leg over the eagle's back. He turned round to see if Eileen had come out of Mrs. Murphy's shop, and gave a cry of terror!

Mrs. Murphy's shop was no longer there! The main street, the chapel, the whole town had vanished, and he was alone with the golden eagle on a bare hillside!

'Let me get off!' he cried. 'Let me get off!'

But with a great flapping of its huge wings the eagle rose – up! up! up! Seamus crouched down among the thick short feathers and clung to the long ones.

'Where are you taking me?' he asked, trying not to be

afraid.

The eagle's wings made such a rush of wind that Seamus did not expect to be heard, but the eagle glanced over its shoulder and shrieked out: 'To THE WISE WOMAN OF YOUGHAL!'

The great bird's beak looked terrible to Seamus, but he could tell that he was out of reach.

'And you pretended not to know!' he exclaimed scornfully.

On flew the eagle, and it was so cold that Seamus was glad to cuddle down and keep quite still.

Seamus dared not look down, but now they were flying in circles, lower and lower.

At last he ventured to look over. Below he saw a lovely little town stretching along a sandy beach at the mouth of a river. A loaded ferry was crossing and the people in the boat stared and pointed up at the eagle.

Some of them were so excited that they sprang to their feet and nearly capsized the boat!

Seamus felt quite proud of himself.

'Wouldn't any one of them wish to be me!' he thought, quite forgetting that he was hidden by the eagle's wings.

They left the town and the ferry behind. The great bird flew slowly, as if not sure of the way. The tops of the trees were close and Seamus was very anxious as he saw that they were descending upon a wild rocky moor, where nothing grew but brambles and blackberries.

'He's taking me to his nest,' muttered Seamus. 'I wonder what eagles eat as well as birdseed?'

And he wished he had never set eyes on the eagle.

The eagle gave three screams, flapped its wings twice, making such a breeze that Seamus was nearly blown away, and came down on top of the highest rock.

With another scream he fluttered to the ground and tumbled Seamus from his back.

Seamus sat up and looked about him.

He had never seen a bird's nest like this before!

In a sheltered corner smouldered a turf fire. Beside it squatted the oldest, dirtiest woman he had ever seen, wrapped in the most tattered plaid shawl imaginable. She was The Wise Woman of Youghal!

'So it's yerself, is it?' said the old woman to the eagle. 'What d' ye mean, screeching like that at a decent woman's door? An' who's that shrimp of a lad ye've brought me?'

The eagle didn't answer. He had his beak in the old woman's saucepan and he was eating away as hard as he could.

She hopped over to Seamus and, before he could escape, caught him by the leg.

'What are you good for?' she asked, peering at him through her tangled hair.

'Jography, 'rithmetic, an' whistlin'!' cried the eagle in a muffled voice, for he wouldn't stop eating for a single moment.

The old woman hopped back to her seat by the fire.

'Jography, indeed!' she jeered. 'Answer me this now. How long must you be flying east before you reach the west?'

Seamus didn't know.

'That for him an' his jography!' exclaimed the old woman, snapping her fingers. 'Let's see what his 'rithmetic is like!'

She sat thinking, with her head on one side, while Seamus did his tables up to twelve times in his head.

'She can't beat me at sums,' he thought proudly.

'If a robin lays three eggs before Easter, how many will a wren lay before Whit?' she asked at last.

'That isn't proper arithmetic!' cried Seamus indignantly. 'We don't learn things like that at school!'

'The boy's nothin' better than an omadhaun!' jeered the old woman. 'Take him away out of that!'

This time the eagle took his head out of the saucepan.

'Whistle!' he commanded. 'Whistle to the woman!'

Seamus didn't give the Wise Woman a chance of telling him what to whistle. He started away at once on *The Irish Washerwoman*.

The eagle stopped rattling his beak in the saucepan and began dancing. His wings outstretched, he sprang up and down, poking his head out, throwing it back, snapping his beak in time to the music.

The Wise Woman danced with him. She flung away her shawl, her hair fell down over her eyes.

Backwards and forwards they went, round and round, until Seamus was out of breath and they were dizzy.

'Is there any more of it?' asked the Wise Woman.

Seamus had whistled the one tune over and over again, but he didn't tell her that.

'As much more as you like, and I know dozens of other tunes,' he told her.

'So now will you tell me where I'll find what I'm seekin'?' screamed the eagle.

'What are you seeking?' asked Seamus curiously.

'The four-leaf shamrock, to be sure!' replied the eagle. 'The one with a dewdrop always at its heart!'

Seamus nearly jumped out of his skin when he heard that. He glanced down at his coat, wondering if he had lost his harp with the four-leaf shamrock Aunt Una had sent him.

Seamus had turned up his collar and the harp was hidden. He peeped inside. No! But his shamrock hadn't a dewdrop in the heart of it!

'Even if it had to start with, it just couldn't be there now,' he decided, and he settled down comfortably to watch the Wise Woman.

She took a handful of grey ash from the edge of the fire and scattered it in a circle round her. Then she squatted down and covered her face with her hands.

The eagle watched her anxiously. So did Seamus.

At last she looked up.

'It was growing on the south side of the third rock of the Macgillicuddy Reeks as you fly west over the Gap of Dunloe,' she said.

'Where in the wide world is that?' screamed the eagle angrily.

'In Kerry!' replied Seamus quickly.

'Well, well!' exclaimed the Wise Woman. 'He knows that!'

'Didn't I tell you?' snapped the eagle. 'Well, I'd best be off. Which way do I go?'

The Wise Woman chuckled.

'Not so fast, me bould bird. It was there. But it's been picked!'

The eagle flung himself on his back and kicked the air, he was in such a temper. When he sat right way up again his beautiful feathers were covered with ashes.

'Tell me who picked me four-leaf shamrock with a dew-drop in the heart of it,' he said sulkily.

The Wise Woman covered her face with her hands once more. This time she spoke through her fingers.

'A woman picked it. She stuck it on a harp and sent

it to a little girl: a little girl with brown hair and grey eyes called Eileen.'

Seamus gave a jump when he heard it was Eileen who had the four-leaf shamrock with the dewdrop in its heart.

'Oh!' he exclaimed. 'Oh!'

The Wise Woman and the eagle both glared at him.

'Do you know where she is?' they asked together.

Seamus sprang behind a rock. 'What will you give me if I take you to her?' he asked, thinking how artful he was.

'Come out of that and I'll show you!' screamed the eagle.

Seamus laughed to himself. The eagle couldn't get at him because the rocks and briars protected him, but he knew he had to watch out for the Wise Woman.

'Listen now!' he said. 'If you promise to get me the finest Easter egg I've ever seen to give Eileen, I'll take you to her.'

The Wise Woman and the eagle burst out laughing.

'It's the little girl I saw coming out of the shop with a silver bird in her hands!' screamed the eagle. 'I'll take her to keep me nest tidy, and I'll tear the silver bird to pieces!'

Seamus was terrified at what he had done. He must be there to save Eileen from the eagle.

'You'll never find her without me!' he said. 'Take me with you!'

And he tried to scramble on the bird's back.

With a scream of defiance, the eagle threw him off and, stretching out his wings, shot up into the air. Seamus watched until the great wings became as small as a robin's. Then the eagle was out of sight!

'Now start to work!' the Wise Woman told him.

'Sweep the ashes, fetch the water, cut heather, and make me a fine soft bed.'

14

Where is Seamus?

n the little whitewashed cabin on the edge of the bog they were all very sad without Seamus.

When Eileen woke up on Easter Sunday morning there was a big cardboard box on the table beside her bed. She knew it held an Easter egg and that there would be one for Seamus too.

'I won't open it until Seamus comes back!' she decided.

'Perhaps he is back!' she exclaimed and, jumping out of bed, ran to see.

But the truckle-bed under the stairs was empty, and she came slowly back across the kitchen, feeling lonelier than ever.

Big Fella the dog whined, and Rose the cat came out from under the table yawning and stretching.

'Where is Seamus?' they seemed to be asking.

No one knew. The turf-cutter and his wife had asked everyone. But since Eileen had parted from him outside Mrs. Murphy's shop, Seamus had disappeared.

'He was very set on going to his Aunt Una's again,' said the turf-cutter. 'Would he have tried to find his way to her place, would you be thinking?'

'Surely Seamus wouldn't do anything so foolish!' cried the children's mother. 'But – just in case – I'll write to her!'

Eileen went out to talk to Long Ears.

'Seamus wouldn't go to Aunt Una's without us, would he?' she asked.

The little grey donkey looked at her mournfully and flapped his big ears as if he were saying: 'Indeed, no! Seamus wouldn't do that!'

The toy aeroplane Eileen had bought at Mrs. Murphy's was inside the tool-shed. Eileen had pushed it in there when they were hunting for Seamus and had forgotten it until this moment.

'If this was only big enough I'd go up in it and soon find out where Seamus is,' she said sorrowfully.

There was a key at the back under the wings. Eileen found the hole where it fitted and turned it round.

'Buzz! Buzz!' went the aeroplane and, humming like a great bee, it shot out of Eileen's hands over the shed and the hedge up into the air!

It flew along over the canal towards the flat-topped mountain.

The sun gleamed on its wings, and Eileen, running down the path, flung open the garden gate and followed along the road.

Before she crossed the bridge the aeroplane was out of sight behind the trees.

Eileen was out of breath. She walked slowly now looking about her. There were buds on the bushes and primroses were growing in clusters under the bracken.

'If only I had Seamus with me now, what fun we'd have,' she sighed. 'And I do believe it was here I saw the leprechaun!'

Eileen stood there, thinking of all the adventures she had shared with her brother and wondering when he would come back. She was so still that an impudent sparrow perched on her shoulder and peeped round at her face.

'What a silly scarecrow!' he chuckled to himself.

'I'm not a scarecrow!' cried Eileen indignantly.

'Tweet-twit!' said the sparrow saucily and flew away.

Suddenly Eileen heard a faint tap-tap! and a squeaky voice singing:

> 'It's tired I am of making shoes!
> I never hear a scrap of news.
> Here I sit and hammer away,
> With never time for a holiday.
> Hammer and sew, hammer and sew:
> Sole and upper and heel and toe.
> Tired I am of all this mending,
> Me with a crock of gold for spending.
> Ready I am to up and away.
> I'm tired of work, it's time for play!'

Eileen laughed to herself.

'If I haven't found the leprechaun again! And, hark at him! He can't sing a note. His voice is all cracked. I'll show him how to sing a song properly.'

And, just for fun, she sang the leprechaun's song right through, from beginning to end.

No doubt about it, Eileen could sing! Anyone would stop and listen to her. When she finished she discovered that quite a crowd had gathered round.

A squirrel with a nut in his paws was peeping out of a hole in the trunk of the tree behind her. On a branch above sat a blackbird, its yellow bill shining, its bright eyes half closed. A robin strutted up and down in the roadway, while sparrows had perched so thickly on the bushes that they looked like leaves.

Eileen scarcely noticed the birds and the squirrel, for with his hammer tucked under his arm and his cap pushed right back, the leprechaun was standing in front of her!

'An' where in the wide world did ye learn that song?' he demanded.

'I heard you singing it!' replied Eileen.

'Is it the same song?' asked the leprechaun in surprise. 'I never knew I sang that grand,' and he looked so pleased and proud that Eileen found it hard not to laugh at him.

'It's exactly the same song,' she told him. 'But are you really going to give up making shoes?'

Without answering the leprechaun quickly snatched the cap from his head and rolled it round his hammer. He pulled off his apron and wrapped them all into a bundle which he laid upon the ground.

Kneeling down the leprechaun put his hands over his mouth and blew and blew and blew at the bundle.

The bundle gave a wriggle. A snout, two small eyes, and two floppy ears came at one end. At the other appeared a curly tail, while underneath four stumpy legs lifted the bundle up from the ground.

'Oh! Oh! OH!' screamed Eileen.

The bundle changed from brown to white and there stood a little white pig!

'You were with us at the Fair!' cried Eileen.

The leprechaun smiled, but didn't say a word.

'If anyone can help me, it's him,' she thought. 'I'm sure it is magic that took Seamus away, and it is only magic can bring him back!'

'I'm sure it was you helped me win that lovely clove walking-stick!' said Eileen to the leprechaun. 'Please help me now to find Seamus. I know you can. You're so clever!'

The leprechaun was delighted at her praise, but he didn't want to find Seamus.

'That's the lad tried to steal me gold on me,' he grumbled.

'He didn't think it was stealing,' explained Eileen. 'And I promise he won't try again!'

The leprechaun twisted his long beard round his neck like a muffler.

'No one could take me gold now,' he said. 'When I give up making shoes I'm safe. There isn't one can touch it then. The torment is I can't touch it meself until I'm back at the cobbling. Isn't it very hard on me? Wirrastru! Wirrastru!'

'So that's why you hadn't any money to spend at the Fair!' exclaimed Eileen. 'But you gave us two half-crowns. I don't understand it at all!'

'Why would you!' exclaimed the leprechaun crossly. 'I never could agree with people that want every happening sorted out and explained!'

He turned away, the little white pig trotting beside him.

'Don't go away!' pleaded Eileen. 'If you don't help me I know I'll never see Seamus again!' And big tears ran down her cheeks.

The leprechaun came back. He was terribly upset at seeing Eileen cry.

'There, there!' he said kindly. 'Don't cry, allanna! I've a wee bit of a gra for yerself, so tell me what mischief this Seamus is up to and I'll see about it!'

'Seamus is lost!' Eileen told the leprechaun. 'And I'll never be happy until he's found. Holidays aren't any good at all without Seamus!'

The leprechaun held his chin in his hand and thought hard.

He took a good look at the squirrel, who was so sorry for Eileen that he had forgotten to finish the nut he was eating and let it fall on the grass.

'Stay-at-home!' said the leprechaun, so scornfully that the poor squirrel shrank back into his hole and didn't dare to put out even the tip of his nose.

The leprechaun looked at the blackbird.

'Gadabout!' he muttered, but the blackbird just tilted his yellow beak and sang softly. Spring made him so happy he didn't care for the crossest leprechaun in the world!

The leprechaun wouldn't bother to give one glance at the sparrows.

'Chatterboxes!' he said to himself and turned to stare at the robin redbreast, who stared back.

'You're the lad for news!' he exclaimed. 'Have you e'er a notion where Seamus is?'

The robin stuck out his chest and strutted up and down.

'Did ye ever hear tell of THE WOMAN OF YOUGHAL?' he asked.

'THE WISE WOMAN OF YOUGHAL?' screamed the leprechaun. 'Hasn't the whole world heard of her!'

The robin jerked his head up and down.

' 'Tis with her me bould Seamus is,' he said.

'I never heard of The Wise Woman of Youghal!' said Eileen, wiping away her tears. 'Will she be kind to Seamus?'

'You never heard of The Woman of Youghal!' exclaimed the leprechaun.

The squirrel was so surprised he came right out of his hole; the blackbird fluttered straight up and down again; the sparrows opened their beaks as wide as they could and sat without making a sound; the robin flapped his wings. Even the little white pig sat on his hind legs and held up his front legs in amazement!

They formed a ring and danced round Eileen, singing:

'Did you never hear tell of THE WOMAN OF YOUGHAL?
    THE WOMAN OF YOUGHAL – THE WISE WOMAN OF
        YOUGHAL!
She lives on a rock, all alone by herself:
She has ne'er a dresser all piled up with delph:
She hasn't a cat, or a dog, or a mouse :
She hasn't a turf-pile: she hasn't a house!
She can tell you the future and likewise the past.
Her knowledge and wisdom are terrible vast.
She's wrapped in a shawl that's as big as a sail.
Her friend is an eagle and that's a long tale!
When she asks you a question you'd better sit dumb,
For always and ever there's worse still to come!
    Oh, THE WOMAN OF YOUGHAL! THE WISE WOMAN OF
        YOUGHAL!'

They stopped dancing and singing and sat down panting.

Eileen looked down on them scornfully.

'I don't think she's wise a bit!' she declared. 'It's terrible silly to live on a rock all alone. I think my mother's ever so much wiser, and better and cleverer too!'

'Well! Well! Well!' exclaimed the leprechaun, looking very upset. 'That's no way to talk about a Wise Woman at all!'

'Sure the child's right to stand up for her own!' chirped

the robin.

The squirrel, curling his beautiful, bushy tail over his right shoulder, nodded so vigorously that he nearly tumbled to the ground.

The sparrows, who hated keeping silent, chattered all together, some saying that the leprechaun was right and others that he was wrong and it was Eileen who was right.

'What's all this noise about?' asked a voice so loud that it could be heard above the racket.

Eileen, the leprechaun, the robin, the squirrel, and every one of the sparrows stopped talking and stared down at the road.

It was empty!

They stared in at the bushes and under the trees, but they couldn't see a soul beside themselves.

'I've been yelling for help until I'm sick and tired of it!' scolded the voice. 'I've never in all my life heard such a lot of noisy, idle creatures! Catch hold of me rope, will yez?'

'It's up the tree!' cried Eileen.

There was a glitter of silver through the leaves. The squirrel darted into his hole; the robin scuttled under a bush; the leprechaun picked up his pig and stood ready to run.

'Hush!' said each sparrow. 'Hush! Hush! Hush!'

'It's coming down the tree!' cried Eileen. 'Oh! What can it be!'

The end of a rope slapped her face. She caught hold of it and held fast.

Something glittering was climbing down the tree – slipping and scrambling and grumbling and making a clatter like a lot of milk-cans tied together.

Eileen was so frightened she shut her eyes.

The leprechaun crouched behind a rock.

The sparrows hid their heads under their wings and pretended to be asleep.

'There's only one had the pluck to stop and face me!' exclaimed the voice.

Eileen opened her eyes.

At the foot of the tree stood a man dressed in shining clothes.

His coat, his trousers, his boots, his cap were like silver, and he wore a pair of goggles pushed back on his head.

He was so thin and his legs and arms were so jerky that Eileen thought he looked more like a grasshopper than anything else.

In one hand he carried a tin of metal polish; in the other a piece of dirty rag.

'Are your clothes really made of silver?' asked Eileen timidly.

The thin man shook his arms and legs till they rattled.

'Stop talking rubbish and tie that rope to a branch!' he snapped. 'D'ye want me aeroplane to fly away on me?'

Suddenly Eileen remembered her aeroplane. She had been so busy thinking about Seamus she had forgotten all about it.

'I have an aeroplane too!' she said proudly.

'I saw it! A sixpenny one out of a toyshop!' jeered the airman. 'Still we can make use of it. It's stuck up there atop of the tree!'

When the leprechaun saw that the airman was friendly he came out from behind the rock and put down his pig. The squirrel, the robin and the sparrows crowded near.

The airman sat down and began shining his boots with the metal polish.

'Maybe you'd give us a hand to get Seamus back?'

asked the leprechaun.

'That's what I'm here for!' said the airman so crossly that the leprechaun jumped nervously. 'But what will I get for me reward, that's what I want to know!'

'I'll give you my aeroplane and my Easter egg!' promised Eileen.

The airman shook his head.

'I've a better aeroplane already, and I can get all the eggs I want while there's nests about,' he said.

The sparrows and the robin didn't like this kind of talk at all.

'I expect he means eagles' eggs!' Eileen whispered, and that made them feel better again.

'I could do with a little white pig!' said the airman, putting his head on one side and looking hard at the leprechaun.

'You'll not lay a hand on my pig!' shrieked the leprechaun, dancing with rage.

'Then I'm going back to me aeroplane!' declared the airman, putting his tin of metal polish in one pocket and the rag in another.

Eileen caught him by the arm.

'Oh, please help poor Seamus!' she pleaded. 'I'll do anything I can for you!'

'What can you do?' he asked.

Eileen tried to think, but she was so bothered that she couldn't remember anything.

'She can sing,' chattered the robin, 'for I've heard her.'

'She can scatter breadcrumbs and bacon rinds, for we've eaten them,' twittered the sparrows.

'She can run and jump, for I mended her boots,' said the leprechaun.

The squirrel rubbed his head with his tail. He wanted

to help Eileen, but he hadn't a good memory at all and could think of nothing.

'I'll give you half of all the nuts I've stored away, if I can find them,' he promised.

The airman sat there, considering.

'Could ye say a piece of poetry – a nice, long piece?' he asked.

'Indeed I could,' replied Eileen. 'I know heaps and heaps of poetry. But won't you wait till we get Seamus back? The poor boy will think he's lost for ever!'

'He isn't lost at all,' said the airman. 'He knows where he is, and so do we. If I bring him back, what poetry will you say for me?'

'I'll say *The Irish Widow's Message to her Son in America*,' promised Eileen.

'Is it sad?' asked the airman.

'It is and it isn't.'

'And what else will you say for me? A job like this should be well paid.'

'*The Battle of Fontenoy*. That's a grand piece, all about fighting, and it's real long,' Eileen told him.

The airman got up.

'Well, the sooner we get there the sooner we'll be back. But I'm not going alone, that's sure.'

'I'll come,' said the robin. 'I'll sit in front and keep watch.'

'I'll come, an' me pig with me,' said the leprechaun. 'A Wise Woman needs careful handlin' an' I'm the one for that!'

'And I'll come, because I've always wanted to fly up in the sky,' said Eileen. 'Besides, I can't feel happy till I see Seamus again.'

'Upon me word!' exclaimed the airman. 'Is it a Noah's

Ark ye think me aeroplane is? A great fat girl is enough without that chap an' his pig, let alone a farmyard of fowl!'

'I'm not a great fat girl!' cried Eileen indignantly.

The airman took out his rag, gave himself a rub all over, and began to climb the tree.

Eileen gave a jump, caught the lowest branch of the tree, swung herself up, and followed him.

When she was near the top she looked down to see how the white pig was climbing.

He wasn't climbing at all! He was sitting down comfortably on a heap of dried leaves. The leprechaun, with his hand to his ear, was listening to the robin, who was chirping softly, with the sparrows crowding round not making a sound.

Even the squirrel was leaning from his hole trying to hear what the robin was telling them.

'Now isn't that robin a dreadful chatterbox!' thought Eileen. 'The leprechaun should know bettter than to stay there wasting time. I've a good mind to go off without any of them.'

But the airman was so queer and strange that Eileen felt she would like some of her friends with her.

The airman made such a rattling and clattering that Eileen couldn't make out anything the robin was saying, and that vexed her all the more.

'You're a terrible slow climber,' he said over his shoulder, and he scrambled into his seat.

Eileen called out so crossly that the squirrel almost fell down.

'Aren't you ever coming?' she asked.

The leprechaun looked up and put his fingers to his lips.

'Sh!' he said. 'Sh! Sh!! Sh!!!'

The sparrows, the robin, and the blackbird looked up at her and hissed softly: 'Sh! Sh! Sh!'

The little white pig flapped his ears and grunted.

'I won't "Sh!" ' declared Eileen. 'Why should I? You're all talking. At least the robin is chattering and the rest of you listening.'

The robin flew up and perched on her shoulder.

'You mustn't be angry,' he whispered. 'I had to tell them first just to keep them quiet. You know what inquisitive creatures sparrows are. But the WREN, the king of the birds, has come to warn us. Look! There he is!'

Eileen saw a little brown bird like a mouse darting among the bushes, going from bird to bird. She could hear a faint 'Sh!' and then there was silence.

She wondered at the way they all obeyed the wren, bowing down and touching the ground with their beaks until he went on.

'What is he warning them against?' asked Eileen, feeling quite troubled.

'The eagle is hunting!' whispered the robin. 'He hasn't been in these parts for years, and he's ragin' mad. He took off Seamus to be a servant to the Wise Woman so that she'd tell him where to find what he's seeking. And she told him – so she did. More's the pity!'

'What is the eagle seeking?' asked Eileen. 'Do tell me, please do.'

'A little girl with brown hair and grey eyes and her name is Eileen!' replied the robin softly.

'That's me!' exclaimed Eileen. 'What can the eagle want with me?'

'He wants the four-leaf shamrock with a dewdrop in the heart of it!' was the answer.

Eileen remembered the harp Aunt Una had sent her. It was still fastened in her coat.

'Oh!' she cried. For just where the four leaves of the shamrock met was a gleaming crystal.

She touched it with her finger, wondering that the dewdrop had not dried up or fallen off.

It was liquid, but when she took her finger away it was still there.

'It can't be a real dewdrop!' she thought.

'If I give my harp to the eagle, maybe he'd bring Seamus back?' she said eagerly.

The robin nodded his head very, very slowly.

'Maybe he would. But would it be wise to give a magic shamrock to a great powerful cruel bird like the golden eagle?'

Eileen sat perched on a branch while she tried to make up her mind.

'If there's magic in my shamrock, why shouldn't I use it myself?' she asked at last.

'Why not?' agreed the robin. 'Let's up and off with us. A clever girl like yerself will surely be able to best the eagle. And think of the friends that's helping you.'

Eileen climbed out into the sunlight. After her came the little white pig, nearly choking because he was trying desperate hard not to make a noise with his grunting, while his master pushed him up from behind.

The leprechaun hadn't any bother with himself. He just trotted up the tree as if he were on a ladder.

At last they were all huddled together, holding tight to the topmost branches which made them dizzy with their swaying, and wondering what to do next.

The airman was passing the time by polishing his machine and grumbling to himself.

'Isn't it terrible to think of muddy boots and sticky fingers and scratchy claws taking the shine off me lovely aeroplane!' he muttered.

'Use yer shamrock!' whispered the leprechaun. 'Use it now and stop that feller's chat!'

Eileen was puzzled.

'I don't know what to do with it,' she said, unfastening the harp from her coat and staring at the withered sprig of shamrock.

The tiny dewdrop gleamed golden, purple, and green.

Suddenly Eileen knew what to do.

Her toy aeroplane was tied to a branch. She touched it with the shamrock.

'Grow big!' she whispered. 'Grow big quickly!'

The tiny aeroplane trembled from end to end. The wings spread, the body swelled, the propeller became larger and larger as they watched.

'In with you!' the leprechaun ordered, and over the side scrambled the little white pig, settling himself in the cockpit, with his snout just showing.

The leprechaun went in next and Eileen sat beside him.

She was turning to ask the airman if they should start when the squirrel swung himself to the top of the tree, gave a spring, and landed on Eileen's knee.

'Who asked you to come?' demanded the leprechaun.

The squirrel couldn't answer for a moment because his mouth was filled with nuts. He dropped these on the floor and fanned himself with his tail.

'Maybe before we're back you'll see I'm worth me room!' he gasped.

The robin perched on the front of the big aeroplane, and, as he folded his wings, the blackbird and all the sparrows came fluttering up.

'We'd best be starting!' called Eileen.

The airman stuffed his tin of polish and his rag under the seat as he looked round.

He wasn't a bit surprised to see how the toy had grown and he was glad as could be not to have a crowd with him, but he had to grumble.

'So you're too grand to come with me!' he growled. 'Wait till the eagle comes, you'll be sorry then.'

Eileen looked up at the sky. There wasn't a glimpse of the eagle.

'Don't aeroplanes have to run along the ground to get a start?' she asked anxiously.

'Not our kind,' came the answer.

The big aeroplane flew off like a huge dragonfly. The sparrows settled themselves on the back of Eileen's and the blackbird snapped the string which fastened it.

For a moment the toy aeroplane dropped against the branches and Eileen, terrified lest they went crashing to the ground, closed her eyes.

She opened them when she felt herself soaring up into the air.

Eileen peeped over the side. There was the wood beneath them, and the canal reflecting the clouds and the two aeroplanes.

The leprechaun took charge of the steering. He pretended not to hear the sparrows, who thought they knew all about flying and advised him what to do.

They each had a different opinion, so it was as well the little man paid no heed to their chattering.

As they passed over the cabin, Eileen saw her mother come across the yard and look up.

Away on the bog her father was cutting turf and Big Fella, the dog, was stretched out lazily on the turf-cutter's coat.

'Won't they be surprised when they know it was me flying over them,' thought Eileen proudly.

'Here he is!' cried the leprechaun.

A shadow fell on them. The blackbird clutched Eileen's shoulder with its claws and the little white pig squeezed close to his master.

High above flew the eagle, his giant wings outspread so that Eileen imagined they covered the sky. The sun glinted on the edges of the browny-yellow feathers so that the bird appeared to have been dipped in gold.

'We're flying as fast as the eagle,' boasted Eileen, trying not to be frightened.

The leprechaun was not happy. He tried to keep one eye in front and to look back at the eagle with the other, and this wasn't easy. But when he saw a great black shadow falling across the clouds, he knew what was happening.

'He's gaining on us!' he grumbled.

Eileen could see the eagle's keen eyes glaring down at her. She shivered, for his wings were shutting the sunlight away.

'How brave Seamus is,' she thought. 'Fancy flying on the eagle's back!'

'Faster! Faster!' she called to the silver airman.

But instead of going quicker he began to slow down until his aeroplane was only a few feet in front.

Eileen unfastened the harp from her coat and gazed at the four-leaf shamrock with its gleaming drop of dew.

'If this is what the eagle wants, maybe I'd better give it to him!' she thought.

The leprechaun guessed what she was thinking.

'D'ye want to have this aeroplane torn to pieces, let

alone the big one?' he screamed. 'D'ye want to be carried off to the eagle's nest? D'ye want to leave Seamus with the Wise Woman for the rest of his life? Because all that will happen if you give up the four-leaf shamrock! An' that's what I'm tellin' ye!'

Eileen quickly pinned the harp back on her coat.

'Now will you tell me what to do, please?' she asked.

The leprechaun didn't answer. The eagle was so close that when Eileen looked up she could see his sharp, hooked claws hanging down and she squeezed up to the leprechaun for comfort.

He winked with the eye nearest her.

'The eagle hasn't caught us yet!' he chuckled.

The silver airman waved his shining arm and the sparrows which were perched around him flew up in a cloud, fluttering just out of the eagle's reach.

The angry bird made a dart at one and closed his beak with a snap.

The sparrow was too quick. It folded its wings and dropped like a stone. When the eagle tried to follow the others flew up, beating his head at the back with their wings, so that he was too confused to know what he was doing.

The silver airman guided his flying-machine in circles round and round the eagle, making all the noise he could.

The toy aeroplane kept straight on. When Eileen looked over her shoulder the eagle and his tormentors were far behind. When she looked again they were just a cloud of black dots. When she looked the third time they were out of sight.

Eileen was so happy at their escape that she couldn't understand why the leprechaun was looking worried. His face was screwed into wrinkles and his brows drawn down in a dreadful frown.

'Are you afraid the eagle will hurt the airman or the sparrows?' she asked.

'Indeed, then, an' I'm not!' he replied. 'But it's at the back of me mind that there's more trouble in front of us!'

Eileen looked proudly at her harp.

'Can't I scare away the trouble that's in front of us?' she asked.

The leprechaun sighed.

'The harp's well enough in its way, though it's the shamrock on it that counts and not the harp itself. But if it's the Wise Woman herself that's getting ready for us, I'm thinking we'd need something bigger an' stronger to best that old one. But my pig an' whiskers! What's this comin' at us?'

A dense black cloud was travelling furiously towards them. It was shaped like a birch broom and a big fist clenched the handle.

'Where's that goin' to sweep us to?' groaned the leprechaun. 'What'll we do at all, at all!'

The squirrel was curled in a ball on Eileen's knee. Now he uncurled himself, reached down a paw and picked up one of his nuts.

'You're a grand shot!' he said to Eileen. 'Take a whack at the cloud with that!'

And he put the nut into Eileen's hand.

The queer-shaped cloud had travelled so quickly that it was only a dozen yards away.

'It would be hard to miss that!' declared Eileen scornfully, and without bothering to stand, she flung the nut.

At once the cloud shrivelled up so that you could hardly see any shape to it at all. The nut whizzed by without touching it and the birch broom grew large once more.

'This isn't a game at a fair,' said the leprechaun severely. 'If we're swept out of the sky, what's going to become of us, can ye tell me that?'

'How many nuts have you?' Eileen asked the squirrel.

He sprang from her knee and searched in the bottom of the aeroplane.

Eileen knew he was a nervous, timid squirrel, so she wasn't surprised when he scratched his head, wrinkled up his soft, downy nose and stamped.

But when he held up one small withered nut, she was worried too.

'Is that all you can find?' she whispered, for she didn't want the leprechaun to scold. 'What's happened to the others? I'm sure you brought ever so many on board!'

She made the squirrel and the little white pig get up on the seat while she searched and all the while the birch broom and the great fist holding it came nearer and nearer.

What Eileen did find was a hole close by where the white pig had been sitting, but there wasn't another nut. They had tumbled out through the hole!

'I must do my best with this,' she said mournfully, taking the withered nut the squirrel was holding tightly in his paw.

The strange cloud was so close that Eileen felt sure she couldn't possibly miss even if it shrank smaller than before, but to make sure she aimed at the knuckles of the fist.

Eileen flung the nut with such force that she swung right round and tumbled on top of the leprechaun, but this time she was successful.

A terrible yell came out of the sky; the fist dropped the birch broom, which burst, and there they were in the centre of a blinding hailstorm!

Rattle! Rattle!! Rattle!!! came the hail.

It beat on the aeroplane. It beat on their heads. The blackbird put his head under his wing, the pig and the squirrel squeezed under the seat. Eileen turned up her coat collar, and the leprechaun pulled the brim of his old hat right down over his eyes.

How cold it was!

Eileen put her hands deep down in her pockets, she wriggled her toes, she hunched her shoulders; but every moment she grew colder and colder!

Her teeth chattered, her nose tingled, and her cheeks felt as if someone were slapping them hard!

That was bad enough!

But as the hail bounced from the leprechaun's hat and whiskers, from Eileen's hat and coat, it fell inside the aeroplane and melted.

Soon the squirrel and the little white pig found it too wet to be comfortable, so they came out shivering and grumbling, while Eileen sat on her feet to warm them!

Suddenly the seat began to sag and gave way under her.

'It's gone soft!' she cried in amazement. 'You'd think it was made of cardboard!'

'There's something very wrong with this aeroplane,' complained the leprechaun. 'I'm terrified it's comin' to pieces on us! Let you do something with the magic shamrock, Eileen, there's the girl!'

The leprechaun was right. The aeroplane was coming to pieces!

The wings were splitting; the body had gaping cracks in it; the propeller was half off!

Eileen had been too excited to remember that her aeroplane, even though it had grown so large, was still only a toy and was made of tin and cardboard.

'It was all the fault of that horrid cloud,' sighed Eileen, wondering what she ought to do.

She laid the harp down and stared at it.

What would Aunt Una think if she knew the adventures her harps had brought with them!

'Please take us back to the real aeroplane,' said Eileen.

The leprechaun shook his head so hard that his whiskers worked loose, and, fluttering back, became entangled with Eileen's hair.

'That's no use at all,' he told her, trying to tidy his whiskers with one hand. 'This outlandish machine can't turn and it can't go backwards. Mend it, Eileen, that's the only way!'

Eileen leaned out and laid the harp on the propeller.

'Tighten up properly!' she commanded, wishing she had Seamus with her, for he was a boy who understood machinery.

The propeller wriggled round and round and was tight again.

'That's the style!' cried the leprechaun. 'That's the style!'

They were all so pleased that the squirrel clapped his paws, the little white pig grunted himself hoarse, the blackbird flapped his wings, and Eileen was quite proud until one of the wings split from end to end.

Quickly she laid the harp on it.

'Join up!' she cried. 'Join up!'

And the wing became whole again.

Eileen made the body of the toy aeroplane stiff, the seat straight.

From crack to crack she went until she was tired. Then she had to start all over again, for as fast as she mended, the machine wore out. Bits were falling from it, and though Eileen worked as hard as she could, the aeroplane wore quicker than she could mend it.

Suddenly the leprechaun gave a shout.

'We're there!' he cried. 'We're there!'

The little white pig and the squirrel wanted to see too, so they clambered up on the seat and, leaning on Eileen, looked over the same side.

'Isn't there the least, smallest, bit of sense between the whole crowd of yez?' screamed the leprechaun. 'Sit down at once!'

He spoke too late. The toy aeroplane tipped upside-down. The white pig, kicking and squealing, dropped through the air, the squirrel tumbled after, but though Eileen was toppled overboard, she grabbed the side and clung there!

The leprechaun couldn't see what was happening. He was fixed in his seat, so he couldn't fall out. He twisted himself round and, with his eyes bulging from his head, tried to see a smooth place for landing.

Wherever he looked the ground was covered with jagged rocks and heather. The only smooth spot was the top of a rock which stood by the sea.

And on that rock the Wise Woman was waiting for them, a birch broom in her hand!

The leprechaun trembled when he saw her.

'Is that you, me fine fella?' she shrieked.

The next moment the Wise Woman tumbled over backwards, for the white pig had come down right on top of her.

With a terrified squeal he rolled off into a corner, but before the Wise Woman could get on her feet down came the squirrel. She opened her mouth to scream and he put his tail into it, nearly choking her.

'Er-er-er!' she gasped.

The squirrel was just as frightened as she was. He pulled his tail out of her mouth and ran to hide himself behind the little white pig.

The Wise Woman was sitting up, when – crash! bang! the aeroplane came to bits and fell in a shower on the rock, while Eileen and the leprechaun descended with a bump!

They sat there rubbing themselves and trying to get their breath.

'I'm broke in pieces!' groaned the leprechaun.

'I'm all bruises!' wailed Eileen.

A boy pulled her to her feet. A ragged, dirty boy, with tangled hair like a bird's nest. Eileen knew she had never seen such a tatterdemalion before, but his blue eyes reminded her of Seamus.

He brushed her down and hugged her.

'Eileen!' he shouted, and two tears ran from his eyes. 'Eileen! I thought I'd never see you again. But you must go away before the Wise Woman catches you!'

'It's Seamus!' screamed Eileen, and she hugged him back.

They were so happy to be together again that they forgot about the Wise Woman until a long, lean, clawlike hand clutched Eileen by the arm and dragged her away.

There she stood glaring at them through her tousled hair!

Under her arm was the big birch broom, and Seamus knew, by this time, that she didn't keep it just for sweeping.

'Who's this trespassing on *my* rock?' she asked, shaking Eileen and not giving her a chance to answer.

Then she grabbed Seamus and knocked their heads

together. After that she threw Eileen one way and Seamus the other.

Seamus had grown used to this kind of treatment. He let himself go flop! and sat down. But Eileen went spinning across the rock and fell on her hands and knees.

Before she could scramble up the Wise Woman took her birch broom from under her arm and rolled up her sleeves.

'What do the likes of you thieves and vagabonds mean by dropping down on a decent woman out of the skies?' she shrieked, standing over Eileen. 'I'll teach ye!'

The leprechaun was pinching himself all over to find out where he was broken.

The little white pig was grunting softly to himself and the squirrel was hiding behind a rock, chattering at such a rate that it sounded as if he were eating nuts with the shells on.

Just as Eileen thought the birch broom was going to fall on her shoulders, the blackbird flew to the highest point of the rock and began to sing.

He sang so sweetly that even the Wise Woman had to listen. She dropped her broom and sat down, rocking herself to and fro, while Eileen crept out of her reach.

'Ochone! Ochone!' sighed the Wise Woman, for the blackbird's song reminded her of the days before she became so wise.

They sat listening, and as the blackbird finished they heard a great racket overhead.

'It's the airman coming for us!' Eileen told Seamus.

The shining aeroplane circled above them, and down flew the robin, followed by the flock of sparrows, who were so proud of themselves they didn't know what to do.

'Did you hear how we beat the eagle?' they asked.

'Scared him out of his wits, we did!'

'Catch me believing that!' jeered Seamus.

'Peck him!' twittered the sparrows. 'Pull his hair! Scratch his clothes to tatters!'

The robin jumped in front of Seamus and held up a tiny claw.

'No squabbling here, please!' he said. 'We're not home yet!'

Luckily the Wise Woman was so tired with all the excitement that she had fallen asleep. The sparrows perched all over her and made rude remarks about her and her nest, as they called her home.

The airman let out his rope and the leprechaun made it fast to a rock. The airman slid down and joined them, leaving his aeroplane circling round in the air.

Seamus stared at him in amazement.

'You're a queer-looking chap,' he said. 'Are you made of tin?'

The airman was so annoyed he started up his rope. Eileen tugged him back.

'Don't take any notice,' she whispered. 'Seamus has got into bad ways through being away from home. He is really a most polite boy.'

'Oh! Oh! Oh!' chirruped the sparrows, pretending to be shocked.

'You're a little girl that tells fibs,' said the robin sternly to Eileen.

'No arguing, please!' cried the leprechaun. 'Into the aeroplane, all of yez, an' let's get home!'

'There's not one of yez that will set foot in me aeroplane till I've had me pay. Let me tell yez that now!'

Every one of them looked at him anxiously.

'What about the poetry you promised me?' he asked

Eileen. 'Is that the kind of girl y'are? Makin' a promise an' then goin' back on it!'

Eileen was terribly ashamed of herself. She had indeed forgotten all about her promise.

'I'll start at once,' she assured him.

The airman sat among the sparrows, using the sleeping Wise Woman as a seat.

Eileen folded her hands, put out her right foot, made her best bow, and recited *The Irish Widow's Message to her Son in America*.

When she had finished she waited for the applause. The children in school and the people when she went out visiting always clapped when Eileen recited that piece, but now not one pair of hands, or paws, or claws gave a single clap.

Eileen looked at each one of them.

The airman was wiping his eyes with his dirty polishing rag; the leprechaun was using his long beard as a handkerchief; tears were chasing one another down the squirrel's furry nose; the little white pig was groaning and sighing; the blackbird, the robin, and the sparrows had tucked their heads under their wings and Seamus was blinking hard and pretending the sun was in his eyes.

'Don't you like it?' asked Eileen, feeling dreadfully disappointed.

'You said it wasn't a sad poem! You know you did!' sobbed the airman, pulling his helmet over his face and rocking himself backwards and forwards at a terrible rate.

'Well, it isn't – not exactly!' explained Eileen. 'But I do know a really sad one. It's a poem that makes me cry when I just think of it. Shall I recite that one?'

'No! No!! No!!!' they shouted in chorus.

Eileen's face was red, her eyes very bright. She knew if she stopped now she'd have to cry too, and she was determined to keep her promise.

'I'll say *The Battle of Fontenoy*,' Eileen told them. 'And, if you don't like that,' she added quickly, 'it will just show how silly you are.'

She began at once, before anyone could say a word.

The airman stopped wiping his eyes. The leprechaun smoothed out his beard and looked very fierce. The squirrel went on crying, because once he started he found it very hard to stop. The little white pig became excited, and when Eileen paused for breath he grunted his hardest. As for the birds – they had never heard anything like it before. Their feathers ruffled, their beaks clashed like swords, and Seamus –

Well, Seamus had forgotten many things since he had been with the Wise Woman. Now he began to remember.

'I want to go home,' he said to himself. 'The very moment Eileen's finished I'm going home.'

When Eileen came to the last line she was so excited that she shouted it out at the top of her voice:

'THE FIELD IS FOUGHT AND WON!'

'Hurrah! Hurrah!!' they shouted and then they clapped. They made such a noise that over in the town of Youghal the people stopped one another in the streets and said there must be something terrible happening along the coast!

And THE WISE WOMAN WOKE UP!

She was so scared that she kept her eyes shut tight and pretended to be asleep, but under her shawl, she twisted her fingers round and round and made a spell to bring back the eagle.

'That'll teach them!' she thought spitefully.

The airman stood up and made such a low bow that his head almost touched the ground.

'Thank you! Thank you very much!' he said. 'That is indeed a lovely poem! And to show how grateful I am I'll sing you a song. I made it up myself!'

'I don't believe that old tin can could make up a song,' muttered Seamus crossly, for he wanted to start for home.

Luckily the airman didn't hear Seamus, but Eileen did.

'I'd love to hear you sing,' she said politely, for she knew the quickest way to get home was to have no quarrelling.

'Maybe you won't think much of it,' mumbled the airman, standing on one leg, putting his head on one side, and biting the corner of his polishing rag.

'Sing it! Oh, sing it, do!' exclaimed Seamus impatiently.

'Sing! Sing! Sing!' they all shouted.

'This is the way it goes!' and the airman began to sing very quickly in a high, scratchy voice:

> 'The robin thinks that he can fly:
> Sparrows flap their wings and try:
> The blackbird sings about the sky,
> But I fly.'

'I've never heard such cheek in all my life!' cried the robin indignantly. 'Everyone knows that I've been flying for years, summer and winter, spring and autum. Fly, indeed!'

'You mustn't interrupt,' said Eileen. 'The airman doesn't mean that, it just comes in his song.'

The robin strutted as far away from the singer as he could without leaving the rock, and the song went on:

> 'The eagle flies above them all:
> His tail is long, his wings are broad.

Of every bird he is the lord:
They tremble when they hear him call.
But I fly higher!'

The robin simply could not keep silent.

'That's quite wrong!' he squeaked. 'The biggest silly out knows that the wren is the king of the birds.'

'Shut up!' shouted the airman and continued his singing:

'The robin says the wren is king.
I call the wren a cheat –'

'Stop him! Stop him!' screamed all the birds, flapping their wings with anger.

'The airman is right!' declared Seamus. 'Everyone knows the wren is a cheat. I've heard about him! When the birds were choosing their king the eagle flew highest, but the artful wren had hidden himself in the eagle's feathers, so when they were high up in the sky he popped out and flew higher still!'

Seamus was quite out of breath when he had finished his story.

'There you are,' said the airman, wagging his head in a most aggravating way.

'Listen to me!' screamed the leprechaun. 'The birds weren't choosing the best flier, but the one that would be best as king. The wren showed he had brains, so they chose him!'

'Besides,' the blackbird pointed out, 'it's better to have a wise, gentle king than a bold, fierce one.'

Eileen sighed.

'They are quarrelsome,' she thought. 'I do wish we were home.'

'They didn't seem to like my song very much,' whispered the airman to Eileen. 'Suppose I give them a bit of a dance?'

He didn't wait for an answer, but, kicking out his legs stiffly and flapping his arms from the elbow, he hopped round and round.

His joints rattled and he danced so quickly that the rattling made a queer kind of music.

'I can dance as good as that!' cried Seamus, and he followed the airman round, trying to imitate him.

The leprechaun thought this great fun, and he followed Seamus. Eileen jumped up and danced behind the leprechaun.

Soon they were all at it – laughing, chuckling, chattering.

They made such a noise that they couldn't hear anything.

'This is the strangest ceilidhe I've ever been to,' Eileen was thinking, when down through the air floated a golden feather!

It rested on the squirrel's tail, and when he looked up, startled, Eileen looked up too.

She gave a scream of terror.

'The eagle! The eagle!'

At that moment the Wise Woman opened her eyes, shook herself, and sprang to her feet, showing that she was very wide awake indeed!

'Where's me birch broom?' she roared. 'I'll teach ye!' And she shook her fist at Seamus.

Eileen was so sorry for her brother that she flew into a temper.

'You naughty old lady!' she cried, stamping her foot. 'Don't you dare touch one of us, or I'll use my magic shamrock in a way you won't like.'

The Wise Woman was so startled that she started back, dropping her broom.

Before she could stretch a finger towards it, the airman made a grab, seized the broom, gave it a whirl round his head and flung it far out into the sea!

Splash! went the broom, and right after it came another splash! For the Wise Woman, with a wail of despair, leaped off the rock.

Up rose the broom and the Wise Woman clinging to it. She held her shawl at arm's length for a sail and the wind filled it But both wind and tide were going away from the shore, and in spite of all she could do, she was quickly carried out of sight.

'Good riddance to bad rubbish,' said the airman, fanning himself with his polishing rag.

Eileen tried hard not to, but it was no use: she felt sorry for the Wise Woman.

'She was real bad, I know,' she sighed. 'But I don't like her to be out on the ocean with only a birch broom to sit on.'

The leprechaun screwed up his face.

'Let you not worry about that one,' he said. 'She'll be back with the turn of the tide and fresher for mischief than ever. We've ourselves to fret over now. What's that beauty up to, can ye tell me that now?'

He nodded at the eagle, who had taken his perch on the big shining aeroplane.

The eagle made a noise like an angry cat, sharpened his beak on his claws and glared down at them.

'He'll rip me machine!' groaned the airman, rattling and clattering with fear.

Eileen began to unfasten her harp, but Seamus was

quicker.

Glancing down he saw to his amazement that his four-leaf shamrock had a glimmering crystal in its centre. It was one of the tears he had shed when he recognized Eileen.

'Here you are!' he called to the eagle, standing on tip-toe and holding up his harp. 'Take this and clear off!'

The eagle peered down.

'The Wise Woman was tricking me,' he thought. 'The boy had it all the time.'

He swooped with stretched head and wings outspread. The birds crouched against the rock. The squirrel and the little white pig squeezed close against the leprechaun. Eileen clutched her brother's hand.

Snatching the harp from Seamus the eagle soared aloft, circled three times, then sped westwards.

'Quick!' screamed the leprechaun. 'Let's up an' off with us before he can change his mind!'

They tugged at the rope, every one of them helping, and pulled down the aeroplane. In they scrambled, piling one on top of the other.

'Me machine can't store such a multitude,' growled the airman. 'Out you go, for a start!'

The white pig was bundling in after the squirrel. The airman gave a push and out the poor little creature tumbled, grunting and squealing.

'Can't we squeeze up a bit and make room?' asked Eileen anxiously, though she hadn't room to breathe.

She knew there were too many of them, but she had grown fond of the white pig and couldn't bear to leave him behind.

'That's soon settled!' chuckled the leprechaun and, leaning over, he tapped the white pig with a twig he carried in his belt.

To Eileen's horror the pig turned brown and shrivelled, his flapping ears vanished, his little twist of a tail faded away, his legs grew limp, and there lay a hammer of gold, an old tattered cap, and a worn leather apron!

She had quite forgotten how the leprechaun had made the little white pig.

'I don't like this a bit!' wailed Eileen. 'I think magic is horrid when it works backward!'

'Don't cry,' said the leprechaun kindly. 'He'll come back the same way next time I get a chance of a holiday, though dear knows when that will be!'

'Hold tight!' called the airman, and whizz! off they flew!

It seemed next to no time when they were over the bog.

The turf-cutter was sitting on a pile of turf, with Big Fella the dog stretched beside him. He was filling his pipe when he heard a cheer from above.

'Why couldn't the pack of yez hold yer noise an' leave the man alone?' grumbled the airman. 'As like as not he'll drop his pipe and break it.' But the airman didn't know the turf-cutter!

He filled his pipe slowly and carefully, took a couple of puffs and nodded at Big Fella before he bothered to look up.

The aeroplane was flying over the cabin by that time!

The children's mother ran out with a rolling-pin in her hand and stood staring up at the shining machine.

'Hurrah!' cried Seamus. 'There'll be something good for supper. That Wise Woman nearly starved me!'

'That's a gran' little house,' sighed the airman. 'Neat, an' clean, yet an easy-goin' kind of place, where a man could stretch himself. Hold tight, now!'

He stopped so suddenly that if they hadn't been packed, someone would have fallen out. They were once more above the trees, and he flung out his rope.

'You're not much of an airman,' said Seamus scornfully. 'You should land on the ground. What do you think the wheels are for?'

The airman swung his fist round, but Seamus was too quick for him. He dodged and was over the side, scrambling down, swinging from branch to branch, before he had finished speaking.

The squirrel went next, then the leprechaun, and Eileen was last of all.

'Good-bye!' she said to the airman. 'When shall I see you again?'

'Sooner than you want, mebbe,' was the answer. 'Easy now!'

Eileen clung tightly to a branch, which bent beneath her weight.

'Will you let me come with you just to enjoy ourselves and not when we'd be tormented with eagles and Wise Women?' she asked.

There was no answer, only a creaking and a rattling. Eileen looked round quickly.

A rusty toy aeroplane was hanging at the end of a string which was tangled in some twigs. The big shining aeroplane which had taken her so far was no longer there.

'Did I dream it all?' wondered Eileen, slipping and sliding to the ground.

The birds had flown away, but through the trees came a faint sleepy twittering that made a song in her ears:

> 'Sleepy head. Sleepy head.
>   Go to bed. Go to bed.
>   Time for rest.

Seek your nest.'

'Ah! Ah! Ah!' yawned Eileen.

The squirrel was in his hole. He had wrapped himself in his tail, but one bright eye peeped out at her.

'Good night, Fluffy!' she said. 'Good night!'

The squirrel shut both eyes.

Eileen's eyes were almost closing, for the twittering of the birds grew drowsier and drowsier:

'Another day
Flown away.
Twilight grey
Steals along.
Hear our song,
Homeward tread,
Go to bed.'

'You are a slowcoach!' exclaimed Seamus, as Eileen reached the ground and sat down on a mossy root.

There stood the leprechaun, his apron tied about him, his hammer under his arm, and his long cap dangling to his shoulder.

'I don't understand,' thought Eileen. 'But it wasn't a dream, that's sure.'

'Do hurry!' exclaimed Seamus, impatient to be home.

The leprechaun took off his cap and bowed low.

'Farewell, Eileen,' he whispered.

Eileen unpinned her harp and thrust it into his hand.

'Mebbe you'd be better at magic than I would,' she told him.

A cold wind blew along the road. There was a scurry of dust and leaves and the leprechaun was gone!

'I'll race you home!' shouted Seamus, and without waiting off he went.

The turf-cutter's donkey

But you may be sure Eileen wasn't far behind.

15

The man from the bog

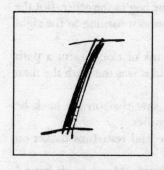

In the summer, when the men were cutting the sods, it never seemed to get really dark. The long, hot days were grand for drying the turf, and all along the stony bog road piles of turf, ready to be carted away, rose like castles, while the freshly cut sods were piled in threes, so that the warm air could move all round them.

Towards evening Eileen and Seamus carried a big can of tea and a basket filled with hard-boiled eggs and slices of soda bread, thickly spread with butter, down to their father.

After tea they all had a great time singing, telling stories, and hearing the news until it was time to go back home.

Sometimes they rode on one of the carts down to the big turf pile on the bank of the canal. All day long the carts were being unloaded, yet the pile grew no larger, for as fast as the carts unloaded turf it was heaped on to barges, which carried it away to the people in the towns.

One morning Seamus was swinging on the gate when he saw a strange man coming across the bog. The cabin was so far from the main road that any passer-by was welcome, and Seamus hoped this man would be a ballad-singer, or a story-teller.

Seamus knew every one of the paths. Not one of them went straight from one side of the bog to the other. But the stranger came straight across without turning to the right or the left.

The sun, hidden behind a bank of clouds, sent a path of light up to the cabin door, and it was this path the man from the bog was following.

As he came nearer Seamus saw that on his back he carried a basket made of green rushes.

The man stopped at the gate and rested his basket on the low, stone wall.

'I am tired and hungry,' he said. 'Many roads have I travelled, many houses have I passed. Now I need rest.'

Seamus jumped from the gate and held it open.

'You're very welcome here,' he told the stranger.

The man bent his head and walked into the garden. Seamus, following, wondered at the queer clothes he wore and at his long, thick hair which reached to his shoulders.

'He's all brown, just as if he were made out of turf,' thought the boy.

The man stood at the door, looking in, and Seamus peeped round him.

That morning, while Seamus cleaned the boots Eileen had been left in charge of the stirabout. She sat on a three-legged stool, just back from the fire, so that she could reach the big iron spoon which stood up in the pot.

For nearly ten minutes she stirred and stirred. Then Big Fella the dog came and sat beside her, so of course Eileen had to talk to him.

'Don't forget the stirabout, there's a good child!' her mother called from the dresser where she was taking down the delph for breakfast.

Eileen gave a real good stir and the thick oatmeal steamed and bubbled.

Rose, the cat, came in from the garden and sat by the hearth.

'Mee-ow-ow!' she said, asking as plain as could be, would breakfast ever be ready?

There was a piece of string on the floor. Eileen picked it up and twirled it between her fingers, making it dance.

Rose never could resist playing with a dancing piece of string. She stood on her hind legs and slapped it. The string swung back and tapped her nose. Quickly Rose stretched out to claw it, over-balanced and toppled on her back, rolling over and over. Springing up, she darted under the table, crouched, waved her tail and pounced!

Eileen rolled the string into a ball and tossed it on the floor. Rose had a grand time with it, and Eileen, forgetting the porridge, sat watching.

'That's a queer smell!' exclaimed the turf-cutter, coming into the kitchen.

'The porridge! The porridge! Oh, Eileen! You naughty girl! It's all burnt!' and Eileen's mother ran over to the fire.

Eileen snatched at the big iron spoon that was sticking up in the porridge and tugged it out. A blob of boiling hot oatmeal fell on her wrist. She gave a scream and dropped the spoon on the clean floor.

'Oh! Oh! OH!' cried Eileen. 'Me arm's all burnt!'

It was then that Seamus and the stranger came to the door. Seamus pushed by and ran to help Eileen. The turf-cutter rushed round and round the kitchen, hunting for the bottle of sweet oil to put on Eileen's arm. Her mother got out an old linen handkerchief and bound it up.

And then they all sniffed. Sniff! Sniff! Sniff! A terrible smell of burning oatmeal filled the cabin.

The turf-cutter picked up the pot and wrinkled his nose.

'There's no eating that!' he declared.

'And there's not another spoonful of meal in the place!' exclaimed his wife.

The stranger stepped forward. He picked up the big iron spoon and took the pot from the turf-cutter. He gave a stir or two – looked hard into it and put it back on the hearth.

'Isn't that very queer!' muttered the turf-cutter. 'I don't smell any burning now!'

'It's me arm that's burnt, but I'm not crying,' said Eileen, trying to be brave, but wanting a fuss made over her too.

The stranger came over to her.

'Let me look at the poor, burnt arm,' he said kindly.

He untied the bandage. Eileen's wrist had been dreadfully red and sore. Now she couldn't see, or feel, a thing wrong with it.

Seamus began to laugh.

'I haven't been pretending, really, I haven't!' protested Eileen.

They sat down to breakfast.

Eileen hated stirabout even when it wasn't burnt. She sprinkled brown sugar over it, when there was any, or milk, or treacle: anything that would alter the taste.

This morning, because a stranger was there, she didn't like to make a fuss. She took a scrap of porridge on the tip of her spoon and swallowed it.

'How strange!' she thought. 'It doesn't taste a bit like stirabout. It's lovely!' And, eating away, she cleared out her basin before Seamus was half-way through his.

The stranger didn't say a word while they were eating, but there was a pleasant, friendly look about him which made them feel they had known him a very long time.

At last they had finished breakfast and the turf-cutter took out his pipe for a morning smoke.

The stranger lifted his basket and laid it very carefully on the table.

'That's beautifully woven!' said the children's mother. 'I don't know that I've seen a finer rush-basket in all my life.'

They all gathered round to look and admire.

The stranger raised the lid. Eileen and Seamus, one on each side of him, wondered what the basket held.

Inside was heather, closely packed. It stretched and heaved up as the pressure of the lid was taken away. The brown man tossed it out and, as the children leaned forward curiously, he smiled down at them.

'What a silly fellow he must be,' thought Seamus, and Eileen sighed with disappointment, for they could see only queer-shaped pieces of bog wood, which their father often found when he was cutting turf.

But the stranger took one out and laid it on the table.

It rolled over, came to rest, gave a little shake and stood up.

'It's a dog!' cried Seamus. 'Did you make it yourself?'

Then he started back, for the dog, though not as big as his fist, seemed to be alive. It wagged its tail, opened its mouth, and stood still again.

'That's a grand bit of carving!' exclaimed the turf-cutter, leaning across the table. 'An ancient, Irish wolf-hound, that's what it is! Wonderful! Upon me word!'

'Oh, the lovely toy!' cried Eileen, stroking the dog

with her finger.

'Oh!' she said again, in great surprise, for the dog wagged its tail.

'Hush!' said the brown man and, opening his basket once more, he took out another piece of bog wood.

'That's a strange-looking thing,' muttered the turf-cutter. 'Where in the wide world did I see a creature like that?'

'It's a dote of an elephant!' declared Eileen, who had ridden on one at the Zoo when she had been up in Dublin.

The elephant rolled his funny little eyes and raised his trunk in salute.

Eileen looked at Seamus and Seamus looked at Eileen. Then Seamus put his finger to his lips.

Eileen knew what he meant and she shut her lips tight, so that not a single word could come out.

The turf-cutter took the dog in one hand, the elephant in the other. Their legs were stiff, their tails were carved from wood, their heads never moved.

'Wonderful!' he murmured. 'Wonderful!'

He held them out to his wife, so that she could look at them too.

Seamus and Eileen held their breath for fear the dog or the elephant might fall. No one noticed the stranger close his basket, smile once more at the children and, with noiseless tread, cross the kitchen, steal out through the open door, into the garden, and away down the road towards the bog.

The turf-cutter turned to speak to him and cried out in surprise.

'I didn't see him go. What in the wide world will he think of our manners, letting him go without a word of thanks or farewell!'

'Run!' said the children's mother to Seamus. 'Run after him and say I wanted to put up a bite for him. Maybe he has a long road to go!'

Seamus darted from the cabin and close behind went Eileen.

There was no sign of the stranger on the road, but Eileen, shading her eyes, thought she could see him climbing the flat-topped mountain.

'No!' declared Seamus. 'There he goes, crossing the bog. He came out of the bog and he's surely going back to it!'

16

The secret road

All day the bog-oak dog and elephant stood on the mantlepiece facing one another. Between them were the clock, which talked the whole time without stopping once, a tin of cocoa, a big spotted shell with the roar of the sea inside, and an old Christmas card.

Without moving they could see these, but the dog could also see out of the window and along the road, while the elephant had to be content with the corner of Eileen's room where she kept her new coat and her best boots.

There they were when the children came home from school.

Eileen dropped her books on the floor, Seamus slung his on the table, and together they rushed to the mantelpiece.

Seamus managed to look properly at the dog by standing on tiptoe. Eileen had to stand on the footstool.

'I wonder if they are only toys,' whispered Eileen.

'Hush!' warned Seamus. 'Wait until dark. There's a full moon tonight.'

Their father had had a long day on the bog. When he came in he brought a creel filled with all kinds of queer things he had dug up when he was cutting the turf with his long, sharp slane. At any other time the children would have been delighted. That was before the man from the bog had given them the dog and the elephant. Now they sat very still and silent, longing for nightfall.

'I wouldn't be surprised to learn that there was a great highway across these parts in ancient times,' said the turf-cutter. 'From that side of the mountain going across the centre of the bog, that's where it would lie. And there's strange tales told of that self-same mountain even in these times!'

At that moment their mother, who was making lace, got up from the window where she was sitting and lit the lamp.

'Time for sleepy heads to be in bed,' she told them.

To her surprise Seamus and Eileen took a drink of milk and, saying good night, went off without a single grumble. Seamus slept in the tiny room at the top of the ladder. He was very proud of having a room to himself, and had stuck coloured pictures on the walls and even on the low, sloping ceiling.

He said his prayers and, without undressing, lay down on top of his bed.

The little window was open. Seamus could hear his father talking to Long Ears, the little grey donkey, his mother calling Rose, the cat, to come in and have a saucer of milk. Big Fella barked as something disturbed him. Two martins, whose nest was under the thatch, chattered sleepily. A bumble-bee, who had stayed out late, blundered into the room, buzzed round, found its way to the window, and shot off!

'Will it never be night?' Seamus asked, and closed his eyes to pretend he was asleep.

It seemed only a moment when he heard a voice say:

'Will we never get that boy awake? Let Eileen come up and try!'

Seamus sat up.

The moon was shining into his room and the window was wide open. He rubbed his eyes and jumped out of bed.

He ran towards the door, but a soft, warning bark called him back.

On the window-sill stood the wolf-hound the man from the bog had taken from his green rush-basket. It was no longer black, and Seamus had never seen a dog to equal it. He was fond of Big Fella, but this dog was so tall and graceful he felt proud to own it.

Yesterday it was small as a toy. Now it had scarcely room to stand on the long sill.

Seamus went over and stroked its head.

'Where did this come from?' he exclaimed, for round its neck the hound was wearing a collar of gold.

Some letters were marked on it, but as Seamus was trying to puzzle them out the hound leapt to the ground.

A thick white mist was rising from the bog, spreading along the road, creeping in at the gate, surging and heaving like a silent sea.

The moonlight made a silver path across the mist and Seamus knew he must travel that path, though he wasn't at all sure that he was awake yet.

The wolf-hound stood with the mist flowing over him; only his head was uncovered, but the letters on his collar shone out clear and plain: BRAN.

'Bran!' muttered Seamus. 'Didn't I learn at school about a hound called Bran? I know, he was the magic hound of Finn, chief of the Fianna!'

'Jump, Seamus!' called an impatient voice. 'We're all

waiting for you!'

It was Eileen's voice, but where was Eileen?

Seamus leaned from the window. A wave of mist tossed up over his head, so that he could not see clearly.

'Jump!' called Eileen's voice again.

'Jump, Seamus! Jump, Seamus! Jump, Seamus!' called so many voices that he was bewildered.

'I can't jump,' he said crossly. 'It's too far.'

'He's afraid!' giggled a squeaky voice from just below the window.

'He's afraid! He's afraid! He's afraid!' whispered voices from the garden, from the road, from the bog.

'Seamus isn't afraid!' cried Eileen. 'Jump, Seamus! Show them you're not afraid.'

It really was a long jump from the window to the ground. In the daytime Seamus would never have thought of trying it. The ground dropped steeply away and the distance was almost twice the height of the cabin.

'I could hold on by my hands and drop. That would be easier,' said Seamus to himself. 'But I won't give them the style of laughing at me!'

He scrambled on to the sill, flung up his arms as though he were diving, balanced himself, and leaped out!

He shut his eyes. He was sure he would hurt himself dreadfully. But no! It was just like jumping on to a feather-bed laid on a spring mattress. The mist gave way, yet held Seamus up, and he even bounced a little.

Seamus laughed and opened his eyes.

Eileen was standing beside him, and the mist, warm, soft, fragrant, rose about them.

'Isn't it fun!' whispered Eileen. 'And you're to lead. There's Bran waiting for you!'

Eileen didn't seem a bit frightened at being out in the

mist. She was always surprising Seamus. He'd think her a gentle little sister that he must stand up for, and there she was always jumping into adventures and thinking it the proper thing to do.

The wolf-hound ran to Seamus and thrust his long nose into the boy's hand.

'You're bigger than you were, old chap,' said Seamus, putting his hand on Bran's collar and following him.

The garden wall had disappeared and they walked straight on to the bog.

The silver path stretched before them. Running swiftly, Seamus and Bran led the way.

Behind them came the tramp of many feet. Once Seamus looked over his shoulder.

'I must be dreaming,' he thought. 'This can't be real.'

Following closely came Eileen riding on an elephant. Its trunk waved aloft and its great feet shook the ground as it marched.

'Who'd believe that great monster came out of a rush-basket,' said Seamus, for he knew this was the elephant which had stood opposite the wolf-hound on the mantel-piece.

He wished he could sit up there with Eileen and look down on the strange procession which followed him across the bog. But on sped Bran, and where Bran went Seamus must go too.

'Bran is the real leader. I am only pretending,' he grumbled.

Every time Seamus looked back he saw a different part of the procession. There were birds and squirrels, the water-rat which lived under the bridge over the canal, there were foxes and rabbits, the leprechaun with his white pig under his arm. Big Fella was there and Rose the cat, carrying her tail on end like a banner.

They were making for the wildest, loneliest stretch of the bog, but every few yards others joined them.

'Where are we going?' wondered Seamus. 'It's a grand leader I am, when it's all I can do to keep up with Bran. Still, I'll keep to the silver path and never let on I don't know anything at all about it.'

Eileen began to sing, and the sound of the marching kept time with her song:

> 'When the moon rides high
> In the summer sky:
> When dreams fly forth,
> West, east, south, north,
> We take the road,
> The secret road.'

The elephant trumpeted and the whole procession sang in chorus:

> 'We take the road,
> The secret road.'

'Now where did Eileen learn that song?' Seamus puzzled. 'I've never heard it before. I'm sure of that!'

Eileen was asking herself the very same question as she sat perched aloft on the elephant.

She had gone to bed just as usual, only far more willingly than on most nights. Nothing had seemed quite the same since the strange man carrying the basket made of green rushes had entered the cabin. And when the moonlight, streaming right in on her, had made her open her eyes very wide indeed she found more differences.

'First of all,' said Eileen to herself, 'there was my nightgown. I went to bed in an ordinary white one, with a skinny little bit of lace at the neck and sleeves. I woke up

in a beautiful lace gown, the loveliest I've ever seen. Then
there was the elephant. All day it was a toy elephant
made from black bog wood. When I woke up it was so
big it had to put its trunk out of the window and it
couldn't go through the door.'

Yet here was the elephant marching along into the
middle of the bog and Eileen, for the life of her, couldn't
remember how the elephant had got out of the cabin.

'Won't it be funny if it can't get back!' and Eileen had
to laugh at the thought of the elephant sitting on the
doorstep or trying to lie down in the garden. 'Maybe,'
she said to herself, 'I'll be able to ride to school on his
back.'

The mist was so thick she could see nothing in front,
and when she looked behind she could no longer dis-
tinguish those who followed her.

'Where does the road end?' asked Seamus of the
hound.

Bran leaped forward silently and Seamus ran beside
him.

'I have never run so quickly before. I must have wings
on my feet,' he thought, looking down.

His feet were bare, for he had forgotten his shoes and
he was dressed in a short, leather tunic.

'When did I put this on?' wondered Seamus.

> 'From nest we fly:
> From beds we hie:
> From woods we creep:
> O'er streams we leap:
> We take the road,
> The secret road,'

sang the marchers.

Bran gave a short warning bark. Seamus held up his hand.

The singing stopped. Only the sound of marching feet went on. Then one after another they came to a halt.

A dark road cut across the path of light. It was walled with white twisted roots of ancient trees which had been dug from near the surface of the bog. They looked like the horns of beasts, but Seamus knew what they were.

On that road shadows, whispering and dancing, darted by. Each one changed its shape continually, a horse turning into a boat, a windmill into a bicycle, a football becoming a swan.

The leprechaun clambered up noiselessly beside Eileen.

'That's the road of the dreams,' he whispered. 'A silly, changeable lot of creatures they are.'

'Can't we go along that road?' asked Eileen.

She spoke very, very softly, but every shadow on the Road of Dreams stood still and stared at her. Then slowly they faded away, although a faint rustle and tiny whispering voices sounded through the mist!

The mist flowed on, blotting out the Road of Dreams with its fence of white twisted roots. It covered the silver path beyond until no trace of it could be seen.

'Oh, dear! What have I done?' thought Eileen in dismay.

The waves of mist rippled over Bran, and now Seamus was almost hidden.

'Seamus!' cried Eileen in terror. 'Climb up to me here. Climb out of the mist!'

Seamus heard her calling, but the wolf-hound leaped forward and he had to follow.

Across the Road of Dreams they went and Seamus felt a drowsiness coming over him. But as they reached the other side he was wide awake.

After them marched the whole procession, and the dreams, sighing and lamenting, fled from them.

Eileen was so high up she could see everything. The mist still rose, but in curls and twists which grew denser as she watched.

'It's like a grey forest,' she thought.

Now she rode on a path winding among trees: giant trees with great overhanging branches heavy with leaves.

'I never heard tell of a wood in these parts,' she said over her shoulder to the leprechaun. 'The only one I know is along by the canal.'

The leprechaun was having a hard time trying to keep his white pig from tumbling off the elephant's back.

At last he settled the grunting, struggling little creature sideways and leaned over it.

Then he answered Eileen.

' 'Twas all a great forest in ancient times,' he said. 'What's the bog itself but dead trees and plants? Didn't ye know that, Eileen? Don't they teach ye anything at all in that stone school house ye're always hopping into?'

'Indeed they do!' Eileen told him. 'They teach us heaps of things. You'd be surprised at all we learn. But I can't be always remembering. Though maybe I will when I'm real old.'

'Maybe ye will,' agreed the leprechaun kindly. 'It's grand to have a power of good things to remember one day.'

Eileen looked about her. The leaves hung motionless on the trees. Long moss was growing on their trunks and birds had built their nests in the branches. But now the only birds in that forest were those who had crossed the bog with Eileen and Seamus.

'Is this a real forest?' Eileen asked. 'It seemed to me that it grew out of the mist.'

'In a way it's real, and yet again, in another way it isn't real,' replied the little man. 'When we crossed the Road of Dreams we came into another land. And I'm a bit of a stranger here meself. But this I do know: Here everything that has been is and maybe everything that will be.'

Sometimes the leprechaun talked so that Eileen couldn't make head or tail of what he was saying, and this was one of those times.

'I don't rightly understand,' she faltered, for she couldn't bear the leprechaun to think her stupid. 'But maybe I will when I get used to it all.'

Now Seamus, although he had to keep up with Bran and so had less time to look about him, had also wondered at this great forest where he had never so much as heard of one.

He had given up asking Bran questions, though he felt sure that the great wolf-hound could answer if he wished, for all he did was to wag his tail or give a gentle bark.

Of course Seamus, being on the ground, couldn't see as much as Eileen, and he had to mind where he stepped for fear of stumbling over roots and fallen branches.

He didn't bother very much, for to his way of thinking, if you were in a forest, you were in a forest, and there was an end of it. But when he knocked against a tree and his arm went into it, the boy was more than a little startled.

'There must be very deep moss growing on that tree,' he told himself.

Seamus was a brave boy and he determined to make sure.

Bran slackened his pace to sniff the air, and Seamus took the chance to poke at the great trunk of a tree with his hand. His fingers sank into it. He could no longer see them, but he could move his hand about as easily as if the tree weren't there at all!

Seamus tried another tree, and his hand went into it as easily as if it were made of mist!

'They're not real trees at all!' thought the boy. 'I knew there couldn't be a forest here.'

But Bran dodged the trees just as if they were real. This made their progress much slower than if they went straight ahead, and Seamus couldn't see any sense in this at all.

'It's silly to behave as if we would hurt ourselves by bumping into these trees. They wouldn't hurt a butterfly,' thought Seamus.

He determined not to trust so much to the wolf-hound, but to lead himself.

'Come, Bran!' he said. 'Straight ahead!'

He put his hand on the hound's collar, and when Bran went to run round a huge oak, Seamus tried to force him through it.

Bran started back and whimpered just as if he had knocked his nose on an ordinary tree growing in an ordinary forest.

He looked up at Seamus with reproachful eyes and shrank away.

Seamus felt terribly sorry.

'I didn't mean to hurt you, old chap,' he said.

'This forest is as real to Bran as the walls of your home are to you!' said a voice beside him.

Seamus turned quickly.

Looking down at him stood the Man from the Bog.

Seamus was as delighted as if he had met his oldest friend.

'I am glad you're here!' he exclaimed. 'Where are we going? And where are we? I began to think I must be dreaming. But now you're here too I know it's real. Eileen! Eileen!' he called. 'Look who's joined us!'

He glanced over his shoulder, but Eileen was hidden from him by the thick branches.

The Man from the Bog drew him on.

'Time enough for Eileen to see me,' he said. 'But we must hasten.'

As he spoke the sound of a horn rang through the forest. One blast! Two blasts! Three blasts! Loud and clear they rang. The forest stirred as though awakening to life. A wind lifted the heavy leaves. Birds sang in the branches. A rosy light shone between the tree-trunks. As Seamus hurried after his companion he struck his hand against the bark of a slender birch. Instead of his fingers sinking into a shape of mist he bruised his knuckles!

'The forest is real to me now as well as to Bran,' thought Seamus as he sucked his hurt hand.

The ground was rising. Ahead went Bran, his nose on the ground, his tail waving. Seamus panted, trying to keep up with the Man from the Bog.

The trees became smaller. The path led through a tangle of briars and stunted bushes. Seamus found his breath coming in gasps. He was tired out and still they climbed!

17

Into the past

he path seemed to end at the foot of a great rock, and Seamus was glad, for he felt he could go no farther.

He leaned against a moss-grown stump when, to his amazement, Bran, with the Man from the Bog following, passed through a gap in the rocks which stood up tall and straight like a gateway.

'I know this place!' cried Seamus. 'I came here a long time ago. Eileen knows it too!'

In some strange way they had reached the flat-topped mountain. It was the little grey donkey who had first brought them there, and Seamus couldn't help wishing he had brought Long Ears with him.

He remembered the Magic Pool and the water-rat who had lived there. He looked about him eagerly, but the Magic Pool was gone. In its place was a great crackling fire of logs.

It was the glow of this fire which Seamus had seen through the trees of the forest. But who had sounded the horn?

The flames rose and sank, rose and sank. Shadows ran

across the grass and hid among the bushes, then sprang up and returned to the fire. Seamus stood there, blinking and puzzled. He longed to stretch himself near the blaze, but something held him back.

Then quite near him a shadow rose and stayed still. Seamus held his breath, for this was the shadow of a man holding a gleaming horn and once more the notes rang out.

They were answered by quick footsteps which approached the fire. Seamus crouched down among the bushes.

The fire sank low and a cloud of smoke hung over it, so that Seamus could see only a faint glow of flame in the centre of a circle of darkness. But, by the light of the moon, which was now rising over the edge of the flat-topped mountain, he could see that the Man from the Bog was no longer with him.

Bran, too, had disappeared; but Seamus was not alone!

The airman, keeping as still as he possibly could, lay in the grass beside him. Now and again a faint rattle, or a tiny clank, told where he was. The leprechaun had settled himself comfortably, using his little white pig as a cushion.

Seamus soon felt an ache in every bone. He hated keeping still, and now a sharp pebble was cutting into his knee, his elbow was resting on a prickly branch of furze, and a feathery blade of grass tickled his nose.

He was determined to see everything that happened, but he felt sure he would have to sneeze or stretch very soon.

'Besides,' he thought, 'I can't see a sign of Eileen or her elephant. I must find out where they are.'

At last he decided to creep round.

He moved gently. The pebble rolled, the prickly furze crackled, and the feathery blade of grass poked into his eye.

The leprechaun caught his arm.

'Don't move, Seamus!' he whispered warningly. 'This is a strange place for the likes of you, and stranger it is tonight than any other time. With so many here that don't belong, I'm desperate afeard something queer may happen.'

'I must find Eileen,' Seamus whispered back. 'I can't leave her by herself.'

'Isn't she with that great big beast of a creature?' muttered the leprechaun, who didn't care for the elephant. 'Let you keep still! Eileen's safe enough. If she is in any danger, aren't we all ready to help? But she isn't. Take my word for it.'

Suddenly the fire blazed up, and between it and the moonlight the whole place was bright as day! Yet Seamus and his friends were well hidden.

About the fire a company of men had seated themselves. They wore tunics like Seamus, and cloaks richly embroidered were flung over their shoulders and held there by enormous brooches. On the ground beside each man lay his shield and spear. Seamus longed to go over and join them.

'They're just like the picture of the Fianna in the big book at home,' he thought.

The Man from the Bog was standing by himself. At the other side was the man who had blown the horn. But he was no longer shadowy. The moonlight made his head gleam white and cold, while the firelight sent a ruddy glow over his cloak and the horn which hung from his belt.

The tallest man was seated on a rock shaped like a throne. He looked about him, and Seamus felt that he must see each one of them, even the squirrel and the cat, who were perched in the crook of a stunted tree.

'Are we all here – Companions of Finn?' asked the tall man.

The man who had blown the horn answered:

'I cannot sound the horn as once I could. Magic works against us and strangers gather where there should be only the Fianna!'

'Are there strangers here tonight?' asked the tall man.

'There are strangers, O Finn!' replied the man who had blown the horn.

Seamus wondered if he should try to creep away, but he would not leave his friends.

'Who are the strangers?' asked Finn.

He lifted his spear, then let it fall again.

'I feared none in the ancient world,' he said. 'I fear none today. How do these strangers come to our gathering?'

The Man with the Horn shook his head.

'I do not know, O Finn. But they are all around us.'

The Man from the Bog stepped forward.

'I bring them,' he said. 'Sometimes I fear that we shall be forgotten. So I bring them by the secret way across the Road of Dreams. I teach them that the past makes the present and the present the future!'

Finn listened with a smile.

'Let me see them,' he said. 'Bring forth your strangers. We do not fear them. We shall welcome them!'

Seamus stood up. His legs were trembling. But he was proud that he should meet and talk with the great Finn.

The leprechaun straightened his cap, drew his fingers

through his beard, and tucked his little white pig under his arm. The squirrel sprang to the ground, then nervously jumped into the tree again.

As they were about to march forward, a strange trumpeting rang through the air. Every one looked at the Man with the Horn, but he stood still. The ground shook beneath a heavy tramping.

The Fianna sprang to their feet. Bran, who was lying beside another hound near Finn, stood up. Only Finn remained motionless and smiling.

'What in the wide world can be making that terrible noise?' whispered the airman. 'I wish to goodness I'd brought me aeroplane! I don't like the look of them lads' spears. They'd make a terrible hole in a man – so they would!'

'Sh!' exclaimed Seamus crossly. 'Can't you see they're not making that noise? It's Eileen's elephant!'

He could see the big flapping ears and the trunk raised above the tangle of bushes and rocks as the elephant forced his way through. At last the great creature burst into the open, marched right up to Finn, and sank down on its knees.

To Seamus's delight there sat Eileen safe and sound. But he was annoyed with her for delaying so long.

'Doesn't she know she should stay with me?' he grumbled to himself. 'She shouldn't stray off picking flowers.'

For Eileen had made herself a wreath of wild roses and in her hand she carried a long rush.

The Fianna caught up their shields and, striking them with their spears, stood in two rows, one on each side of their leader.

'This must be a great foreign princess with her magic

steed,' said Finn.

Reaching up, he lifted Eileen to the ground and put her on the rock throne beside him.

The airman sat up. The leprechaun set down his white pig and the squirrel chattered with excitement.

Seamus expected Eileen to explain at once who she was. He hoped she would say it quickly, for he was impatient to go over to the fire and join the Fianna.

To his amazement she sat there not saying a word, but just smiling up at Finn and looking like a fairy with her crown of flowers and her lovely lace frock.

'Eileen can't want to pretend she's a princess,' he muttered.

But that's just what Eileen was doing.

She hadn't meant to – at first! It was such fun, riding about on an elephant, and her dream frock was so beautiful that she was proud and excited.

It would never have happened if she had been wearing her cotton night-gown or her ordinary school frock. Afterwards Eileen blamed it all on the lace dress, and it's almost certain she was right.

'It's a shame I can't do this every day,' thought Eileen discontentedly. 'I have to live in a tiny little house, and help to wash delph and learn to darn and sweep and cook, when I might be having a lovely time like this always.'

Then she thought how much nicer she would look if she tied her hair up with a bow.

There was no way of getting any ribbon, so, as the next best thing, she made herself a wreath of flowers.

Even the airman thought Eileen looked lovely. And the leprechaun didn't see why she shouldn't be a princess if she wanted to.

But the Man from the Bog was ashamed of Eileen.

'I never dreamt she'd behave this way,' he said to himself. 'I'm terribly disappointed. She isn't at all the child I thought she was.'

'That's a beautiful dress you're wearing, princess,' he said, speaking over the shield of the tallest of the Fianna.

Everyone stared at him and Eileen was puzzled.

'Doesn't he know my name is Eileen?' she thought. 'Still, maybe he thinks it's "Princess", too.'

'Oh, I've heaps of dresses better than this,' she bragged.

'Maybe you wouldn't mind telling me who made it?' asked the Man from the Bog.

Finn and the Fianna and the Man with the Horn looked at him in surprise, for they felt he was being rude to their grand little visitor.

Eileen tried to think. She didn't know. She wished the Man from the Bog hadn't asked her. How could she say that she went to sleep in a cotton night-gown and woke up in a lace frock !

She looked down at it. How was it she hadn't noticed before – that the lace was the kind her mother was always making? No one else could make it so beautifully.

'I don't know who made the frock,' she replied. 'But my mother makes lace just like it. And she's the best lace-maker in the whole of Ireland.'

'And where does this wonderful lace-maker live?' asked the Man from the Bog.

Eileen looked at him in astonishment.

'You know !' she cried. 'It's the cabin at the edge of the bog where the path goes down to the cross-roads.'

'Now isn't that a queer place for a princess to be living,' said the Man from the Bog.

He didn't laugh, but he wrinkled up his face until it

looked like a piece of bark and his two eyes danced in his head with fun.

Eileen's face grew very red. She wished she had never pretended to be grand.

When Seamus saw how miserable she looked he was sorry for her. He jumped up, scratching himself on the furze, and ran over to the fire.

The moment he reached the nearest man of the Fianna, Seamus stood still. He could go no farther. His legs refused to carry him. Slowly he sank down beside a big fat man with a bald head.

Eileen saw Seamus, and was slipping from her seat when Finn laid his hand on her arm.

His touch was cold and damp. She was frightened, remembering the mist through which they had come.

But his voice was kind and friendly, like her father's.

'Stay, Eileen!' he said. 'You and I must act as judges. Let the Fianna see if their limbs have grown stiff and their weapons rusty.'

'A combat! A combat!' shouted the men, flinging off their cloaks.

The fat bald man rose slowly. While the others pulled their swords in and out of the scabbards to see if they could be drawn easily, examined the blades and hafts of their spears, he gathered up the cloaks, piled them into a heap and sat down comfortably on them.

'He's not much of a warrior,' thought Seamus scornfully.

'You lazy fellow!' exclaimed Finn, half sternly, half laughing. 'Have you forgotten the deeds of other days?'

The bald man wasn't the least bit put out.

'That I haven't,' he replied. 'Nor have I forgotten the feasts. This is a hungry, empty land we have reached.

Feasting before fighting was ever my rule!'

'You speak truth, O Conan,' laughed Finn, and the Fianna laughed with him. But Conan frowned, and though he said nothing, Seamus could see that he was angry.

Seamus was curious. The leprechaun had crept closer and he whispered to him: 'Why do they laugh at this fat man?'

'He was always greedy and won his victories by cunning rather than by courage. They named him Conan the Bald!' whispered back the leprechaun.

They spoke so softly that Seamus did not dream they could be overheard, but Conan had quick ears.

He glared wrathfully about him. The leprechaun twisted back into the shelter of the bushes, but Seamus wouldn't try to hide.

Conan stretched out his huge hand and, seizing Seamus by the neck, held him up and shook him.

'Who brought this whispering midget here?' he demanded. 'Am I to have no peace at my own fireside?'

'For shame, Conan!' said Finn sternly. 'Have you forgotten the rules of the Fianna? Put down the child!'

Conan obeyed, but so roughly that Seamus tumbled over. Finn picked him up and set him on his feet, giving a friendly smile which made the boy flush with pleasure.

'What brought you here?' asked Finn.

' 'Twas I brought him,' said the Man from the Bog.

'Let the lad speak for himself!' ordered Finn.

Seamus stood up very straight.

'I didn't know where I was coming,' he replied. 'But I'm glad I came. I want to join the Fianna!'

Eileen felt proud of her brother, but he looked so small and young standing there before those big, tall men, that she feared they might be angry.

The Man from the Bog looked sad and shook his head. Conan looked angrier than ever, but the others raised their spears and saluted Seamus. The Man with the Horn blew a great blast and Finn leaned back in his seat, looking well pleased.

'Such were the boys of our time,' he said. 'But it will be many years, Seamus, before you can pass into the Fianna. Do you know the tests?'

Seamus shook his head.

One of the Fianna stepped forward. He was tall and slight. His hair, golden like Finn's, fell to his shoulders in thick curls. His spear was wrought with gold, and the haft was so cunningly carved that each inch of it contained many pictures.

'Seamus must know the poems of Ireland and be able to recite the deeds and stories of his race,' said this warrior in a voice that was like music.

Seamus made a face. He couldn't help it, but he was terribly bad at learning poetry.

'I'll try,' he said. 'Maybe I'd better begin on the stories.'

Another of the Fianna stepped forward. He had broad shoulders and limbs like trees. In his hand he held a stick which quivered and twisted as if it were alive.

'If you were put into a hole with a shield and a stick you must be able to defend yourself against nine warriors,' he told Seamus.

Eileen had a hard task keeping silent, but she bit her lips and held the words back.

'Nine against one!' exclaimed Seamus. 'But that's not fair!'

The man laughed, put the stick into the boy's hand,

and stepped back among the others.

A warrior whose long hair was in many plaits next spoke. 'With your hair woven into braids, Seamus, you would be chased through the forest. If we caught you, if a hair of your head moved, or if you broke a dry twig underfoot, you could not join the Fianna.'

Seamus had to laugh then, so did Eileen, so did Finn, and every one of them about that fire on the flat-topped mountain, for Seamus had had his hair cut only the day before, and it was cropped short and smooth.

'I can run!' said Seamus. 'I'm one of the best runners in these parts.'

A man with very long legs and keen eyes spoke now.

'Can you leap over a spear held level with your eyes, Seamus? Can you run at full speed under one held level with your knee? Can you draw out a thorn from your foot while you are running? Can you do these things, Seamus?'

'I'll practise,' said Seamus.

Finn lifted his spear and held it out to Seamus.

'Don't touch it!' whispered the leprechaun. 'Don't touch it!'

'Don't touch it!' whispered the Man from the Bog.

Eileen heard them, but Seamus was looking at Finn and did not hear.

'When you can break that spear,' said Finn to Seamus, 'you will be old enough to start on the tests of the Fianna.'

The spear was as long as a tall man, as thick as a well-grown sapling, and it was said to be so heavy that with one end resting on the ground a man who was not in the Fianna could not lift the other end.

But when Seamus put his hands about it he felt it as light as a feather.

He did not lift it. He stood there, gazing at Finn with fear and sorrow in his eyes.

For though the spear seemed as mighty as in the days when Finn had used it against his enemies, when Seamus went to hold it his fingers sank into the wood and clasped nothing.

He thought of the trees in the magic forest, and of how they had become real at the sound of three blasts of a horn.

Seamus looked at the Man with the Horn.

'Sound three blasts!' he said.

The man raised his horn to his lips, but before he could sound a single blast, from far away came a warning cry:

'Finn! Hasten!'

'My comrades call me,' said Finn.

His voice was faint and thin. He stood up tall and straight, but Seamus could see the rock throne through him. He looked at the others. Wavering shapes of mist hovered about the fire, which was dying down.

'Why did you touch the spear?' sighed the Man from the Bog.

'Weren't you warned?' exclaimed the leprechaun crossly.

'Sound the horn!' implored Seamus. 'Sound the horn!'

He shivered with cold. The mist was round him once more. He was terribly sleepy. He yawned and rubbed his eyes.

'Did you hear that?' asked Eileen.

Seamus stared in amazement. He was once more in the kitchen at home. The door stood wide open and the room was filled with a thick white mist.

The fire still glowed on the hearth. There was Eileen, sleepy and her hair rumpled, with her head on one side, listening.

From far away came the sounds of men marching, of spears clashing and voices singing:

> 'A spear, a shield, and a fearless heart
> And a love of our ancient sireland!'

The voices died away.

'Could you hear what they were singing?' asked Seamus eagerly. 'Eileen! Who were they?'

Eileen looked up at the mantelpiece. There stood the bog-oak elephant and the hound, one on each side of the clock, small and still as toys. She looked down at her night-gown. It was the plain white one she had put on before going to bed. She ran to the door and looked out. Seamus looked over her shoulder.

Dawn was rising over the flat-topped mountain. The mist was thinning. The songs of larks rose high in the air. Spears of light were flung across the sky and on the path lay an ancient, rusty spearhead.

Seamus picked it up.

'We know the way,' he said to Eileen. 'We'll see them again.'

Eileen smiled up at the elephant. His little eyes twinkled, but he gazed far away. Would she ever ride again on his back across the Road of Dreams into the Magic Forest?

18
Across the bog

eamus was going to drive his mother and Eileen to the Fair. But Eileen sneezed twice, and when she thought of the great fat book of stories her aunt had sent her for Christmas, she said she was sure she had a cold and would like to stay in by the fire.

The turf-cutter had to go to the other side of the bog, so after breakfast Eileen was left alone in the cabin.

She wasn't quite alone, for although Big Fella as well as Long Ears had gone with her father, Rose was stretched out before the fire.

Eileen thought it great fun to wash up by herself. She made the place look tidy and felt very proud. She had a game with Rose until the ball rolled under the dresser and wouldn't be poked out.

Then she tucked herself into the big armchair and read the first story in her book.

The cabin was very quiet. Rose was busy washing herself. The fire was hot and the wind, blowing across the bog, made a wild music that caused Eileen to look up from her book and sit listening.

She leaned back against the cushions, wondering about

the wind. It was seldom far away from the bog. They knew the direction it came from and the way it was going, but no one ever saw it.

Louder and louder sang the wind! Eileen's eyes closed and she fell fast asleep.

Eileen was awakened by a scratching at the door. She sat up, wondering where she was, for she had been dreaming about the Tinker Chief and the ballad-singer, and it was hard to remember quickly that she was home again.

The fire was glowing, but while she had slept the short day had ended and darkness had crept all round the cabin.

The stew which had been left in the saucepan was giving out a savoury, appetizing smell, and Eileen suddenly felt hungry.

It was a long, long time since breakfast. She must have slept for hours!

She knew that her mother and Seamus would not be home until late, but her father had intended to return for dinner.

Eileen dared not move, for the scratching at the door kept on and she was so scared she could only hope that if she stayed quiet nothing would happen.

But she was sitting on her foot, and it was pricking with 'pins and needles' so that she could hardly bear it.

Then from outside the door came a soft whining and several short, sharp barks.

'Why, it's Big Fella!' cried Eileen, and jumping from the chair, she ran to the door and flung it open.

In came Big Fella, and with him came a white chill mist which blotted out the garden and the road.

'How dark and cold it is,' grumbled Eileen, trying to

close the door.

But Big Fella would not let her. He stood on the step, half in and half out. He looked up at Eileen, and she knew he was trying to give her a message.

'What is wrong, Big Fella?' asked Eileen, shivering as the mist entered the kitchen.

'Wuff! Wuff!' replied the dog, seizing her frock in his teeth and tugging her towards the door.

'Let me close the door,' pleaded Eileen, trying to shake herself free.

But Big Fella only tugged the harder.

'Something must have happened to daddy,' thought Eileen.

She looked out at the mist with frightened eyes. What could she do? She did not know where her father had gone. She would never find him in the dark. If only her mother and Seamus would return!

Big Fella tugged her as far as the step.

Suddenly Eileen determined to be brave.

'Wait!' she said. 'I am coming! But I must bring the lantern!'

Big Fella understood. He sat down patiently while Eileen lit the big storm lantern, slipped on her coat and looked round to see that no harm could come to the cabin while she was away.

Never had the kitchen looked so delightful! Her stocking was hanging at one end of the mantelpiece, Seamus's at the other. The big candle stood in the window, unlit, but gleaming in the light from the fire. The big grandfather's clock and all the pictures were framed in holly and the air was fragrant with the smell of spice and herbs. Eileen sighed as she turned to venture into the chill mist.

Her story-book was lying on the chair. Although she

felt it foolish to take it, Eileen could not bear to leave it behind. Tucking it under her arm she followed Big Fella out of the cabin.

'Good-bye, Rose! You're in charge!' said Eileen as she pulled the door behind her.

Holding up the lantern so that it made a path of light, Eileen followed Big Fella step by step.

The lantern bobbing up and down made such strange shapes on the mist that Eileen was terrified to look at them and longed to return.

Now they were out of the garden on the road. Big Fella turned to the left and Eileen knew they were going right into the bog.

The mist grew thicker. The light was reflected from frozen pools, and Eileen longed to walk beside Big Fella, her hand on his collar, just for company.

But the track they followed was narrow and stony, and she dared not do anything but follow where the dog led – his head down, his tail sticking up.

Eileen was getting tired when she heard a noise behind her.

'Big Fella!' she whispered. 'Big Fella! Stop! Do stop!'

Big Fella took no notice. He trotted on and, trembling so that her teeth chattered, Eileen was forced to follow.

Someone was crashing along the track. She heard a tramping and grunting and a queer laugh!

'There must be nearly a dozen of them,' thought poor Eileen.

She tried to look over her shoulder, but she slipped off the path into a half-frozen pool. Big Fella gave a warning bark and, with eyes staring straight ahead, she ran on.

Once she was sure a muffled voice called her. She was so startled she tripped and let the lantern fall.

Eileen scrambled to her feet at once and Big Fella ran back and licked her hand encouragingly.

'Can't you hear them?' she whispered.

But Big Fella trotted on.

After a while Eileen felt the mist was a protection.

'I can't see them, so they can't possibly see me,' she told herself. 'Besides, if they wanted to hurt me they would have tried, and they haven't. I'm not going to be scared any more.'

Now a bitter wind blew across the bog, changing the mist to sleet. Eileen hated sleet; it was so harsh and unfriendly. The wind changed and the sleet turned to snow, falling straight and steady.

Yet as the light of the lantern flared up Eileen saw that each flake danced and swayed, and no two of them seemed to be the same shape or size.

Watching them Eileen forgot her fear, forgot why she was trudging along in the dark and cold until Big Fella, darting quickly ahead, barked joyfully and her father's voice hailed her.

'Who comes there? Be careful! I am on the edge of a cutting!'

'Daddy! Daddy! It's Eileen!' she called back, holding the lantern high above her head.

She could see her father lying on the ground, the snow piling up around him.

Eileen flung herself on the ground beside the turf-cutter.

'Are you hurt?' she asked in terror.

'Just a twisted ankle, my brave little girleen! I sent Big Fella for help, hoping that your mother and Seamus would be home. I left Long Ears over at the Reardons'. So I'm afraid we'll have to try again!'

'I'll write a note and tie it to Big Fella's collar. Then Seamus will know what to do,' said Eileen, proudly pulling out her new pencil. 'They're sure to be back from the Fair now, and we don't want to spend Christmas on the bog, do we, daddy?'

'That we don't!' replied the turf-cutter, looking curiously at the book, which Eileen carefully stood on end to keep dry.

Off went Big Fella once more. Eileen put the lantern near her father to make him warm, and began to build a turf wall to shelter them from the wind.

She was so busy she did not notice what was happening until her father cried out.

Eileen glanced round, thinking that Big Fella had returned.

She was so surprised at what she saw that she stood hugging a sod of turf and wondering if she were still at home, dreaming in the big chair by the fire.

The book had grown bigger and bigger, until it reached to the branches of a twisted oak which grew by the cutting. Slowly the cover opened like a door and Eileen could see the pictures moving, and those who were in them began to step out, jostling one another and staring around in amazement.

A small dark man, dressed in skins, carrying a leather bag on his back and with a stone hatchet in his hand, came first.

He peered in front, without seeing any one, and talked to himself.

'Here we made the path through the forest. I can't see it now for the darkness, but I know it's there.'

Bending low, he ran along the track and disappeared.

Eileen did not watch his going. She was too interested in the other people in her story-book who were coming to life and greeting each other.

19
Out of the book

 ileen had read only the first story in the book, but she had looked at all the pictures and knew each one of those who crowded out as well as she knew the people in the villages near the bog.

It was grand to see Brian Boru bowing to Robert Emmet, while Queen Tailte gazed in wonder at St. Patrick. Four beautiful swans peeped around the cover of the book, and Sarsfield stood alone, leaning on his sword.

He was the one Eileen admired the most of all, and she was timidly putting out her hand to touch him when she heard Seamus calling.

In a moment the great company were back in their pictures. The book closed, grew smaller, and Eileen was so excited that she did not notice that the little dark man had not returned to his place in the book.

'Here's a way to spend Christmas Eve!' cried Seamus as he sprang down from Darkie's back and bent over his father.

The turf-cutter, who had fallen asleep, woke up.

'It was lucky you sent Big Fella!' exclaimed Seamus. 'When we got home and found Eileen gone we were scared. I set off to find her, but I followed a will-o'-the-wisp and went astray. I've been wandering over the bog for hours!'

'Oh!' cried Eileen. 'I heard something following me a long way back. I was scared!'

'So you were the will-o'-the-wisp,' laughed Seamus. 'You little duffer! Why didn't you call out?'

The children helped their father on to the pony's back. Eileen got up behind him, Seamus and Big Fella running at the side, and back across the bog they went.

The Christmas candle sent its light out through the falling snow.

Eileen was in bed before she remembered her book. Where had she left it? She had seen it beside the lantern as Seamus rode up – its green and gold cover gleaming in the dim light. Had she brought it home?

'If I left it out in the snow it will be destroyed before morning,' thought Eileen anxiously. 'Oh! Wasn't I the silly girl to take it out at all!'

She could not wait. She would never be able to sleep unless she knew what had become of her story-book. The little felt slippers her mother had made for her were beside the bed. Drawing them on and throwing her coat over her shoulders, Eileen ran into the kitchen.

The fire glowed red. The Christmas candle burned with a soft clear glow. The stockings hanging at each end of the mantelpiece, which had been limp and empty when Eileen went to bed, were bulging now. From the top of one poked a doll's fair, curly head. From the other two wheels of an engine stuck up.

Instead of rushing to her stocking and seeing what else was in it, Eileen stood in the doorway too startled to move!

Her story-book was on the footstool, and, crouching

beside it, was the little dark man who had disappeared on the bog.

Rose and the squirrel were asleep in the basket. Big Fella was in the stable with Long Ears and Darkie. Every one else was asleep and Eileen wondered what she should do.

'Maybe if I open the book at the right picture he can get back,' she thought and tiptoed across the room.

In spite of her efforts to make no noise the little dark man heard Eileen, and with a terrified glance over his shoulder he sprang towards the door!

The latch was down, but he seemed to slide through the crack. Eileen opened the door quickly, but there was no trace of the little man!

Eileen went back to the fire and, taking down her stocking emptied it on the hearth-rug.

'I suppose I should wait until Seamus is up,' she murmured to herself.

But she could not bear to go back to bed and she was sure it would be a long time until dawn.

Rose woke up and stalked over to see if by chance there was something for her in the stocking. She would have liked a game with the wooden animals in the Noah's Ark, or the three white ducks, but Eileen put them quickly back again.

She sat stroking her new doll's hair and then opened a tin box labelled 'Biscuits,' but a Jack-in-the-box sprang out at her.

There were so many surprises in that stocking that before Eileen had looked at half of them she fell asleep.

When Seamus came running out as the big clock struck One! Two! Three! Four! Five! Six! SEVEN! Rose was lying on top of the doll and Eileen was rubbing her eyes and wondering how she had got there!

Captain Cassidy and Tim Quinlan, who was now mate on the turf-barge, met them outside the chapel after Mass; and wasn't Seamus proud to drive them home!

The captain had sent a turkey along for the dinner and Tim Quinlan brought his own welcome, for he could whistle every tune he had ever heard!

They had a grand dinner with Rose and Big Fella to help, while the pet squirrel woke up and came out of the basket when he heard them cracking nuts.

All the time they were eating and telling jokes and stories Eileen kept thinking that someone was looking at her through the window. She sat with her back to it, and several times she turned quickly; but could see no one.

'It must be the robin looking for crumbs!' she decided.

So when her mother told her to shake the tablecloth she went to the front instead of the back.

The robin had eaten so much already that he sat on the wall chirping to her and wouldn't bother even to look at the crumbs.

Eileen neatly folded the cloth and then stood staring at the track of little bare feet in the snow, leading from the gate right up to the window!

'It's the little dark man!' she whispered, feeling terribly scared.

Then she thought of him cold and hungry in a strange place at Christmas time.

She tiptoed into the kitchen and cut a thick sandwich. She wrapped this as well as a piece of pudding in paper and, running out once more, put the package on the wall by the gate.

As she was coming back to the house she pulled open the door of the shed where her father kept his tools. In one corner were dry sacks and a pile of hay. Even on a cold winter night the little dark man could keep himself warm there.

'What in the wide world is the child doing?' asked the turf-cutter. 'She'll catch her death of cold!'

'Put on your coat, Eileen!' called her mother.

Seamus ran out with it to her.

'Let's build a snowman!' he said. 'Then we can pelt him with snowballs!'

As Seamus went to get the spade to make the snowman Eileen saw a small hand with long nails reach round the post of the gate and snatch at the food she had left there.

At once she felt happier. She helped Seamus build the snowman. The captain gave them an old pipe to stick in his mouth and Tim Quinlan perched his own hat on the top.

'Now for the snowballs!' cried Seamus.

They made a great pile of them.

Tim Quinlan chose a big one, but instead of throwing he stood holding it and gazing in a puzzled way at the garden.

Eileen knew at once what he had seen – the print of little bare feet in the snow!

It would never do for Tim and the captain to know about the stranger. Snatching up a handful of snow, without stopping to form it into a proper ball, Eileen let fly at Tim.

The snow caught him on the ear and showered over his face and down his neck. At once he forgot the queer marks he had seen in the snow!

As he rubbed the snow from his eyes and poked his handkerchief inside his collar, Seamus roared with laughter at the faces he made.

Eileen watched Tim's face anxiously. Suppose he flew into a temper! But he only laughed and shook his fist at her.

'Ye little rapscallion!' he roared. 'So it's a snow-fight ye want! Come along, then!'

It was easy to see that the track from the gate to the window was forgotten.

Seamus was a splendid shot. So was Eileen. But this time all her balls went into the garden. Seamus was amazed at her. If he or Tim threw a snowball at her, instead of one coming back at them she sent it across to the front of the cabin.

'Your fingers must be made of butter!' he said scornfully.

Eileen didn't care. By the time they were all powdered with snow and were hot and panting, no one could have guessed that someone with bare feet had walked from the gate to the window!

'I'll try to let him have something hot to eat before I go to bed,' thought Eileen as they went into the house.

After tea the turf-cutter and his wife, the captain and Tim sat at the table playing cards. Seamus squatted on the floor building a railway, while Eileen curled up in the big armchair with her story-book.

She turned the pages, but she did not read. She did not even look at the pictures. She was thinking too hard.

At first Eileen had thought of nothing but how to help the little dark man to get back where he belonged. Now she wanted to talk to him – to find out all he could tell her.

'He'd know wonderful stories,' sighed Eileen to herself. 'They'd be better than any I could read.'

There was soup for supper! Thick, hot soup with slices of toast to break up in it. While her mother was serving it, Eileen slipped into the pantry. There was a hole in the corner by the grating and the turf-cutter had fitted a piece of stone into the hole. Eileen filled Rose's saucer with hot soup and, shifting the stone, found that there was just room for the saucer in the hole.

As she poked through a slice of toast and shifted back the stone, her mother came looking for the cat's saucer.

'Have you seen it, Eileen?' she asked.

Rose trotted round and round her feet, purring loudly and saying as plainly as she could that she wanted her soup quickly.

'Did you see it?' repeated the children's mother.

Eileen frowned, but did not answer. She feared it was going to be very difficult to take care of the little dark man.

'Don't worry, dear,' said her mother. 'I may have mislaid it myself.'

'Maybe I'd better let him go back,' thought Eileen sadly.

Rose was given her soup on a tin plate and she didn't like it a bit. She splashed soup all over the hearth and even tried to steal some of Big Fella's, though there was plenty for everyone.

'You'd think Rose knew a stranger was using her saucer,' murmured Eileen as Rose looked at her reproachfully and rolled over on her back.

'It's very strange!' said the children's mother. 'Rose had her saucer this morning. I remember now.'

'I know where it is!' cried Seamus suddenly. 'It's in the pantry: I put it there when I was drying up!'

He ran to look for it, but came back empty-handed.

'Didn't you see it there, Eileen?' he asked.

Eileen grew very red, but bent over her food and pretended not to hear.

'Fancy making such a fuss about an old enamel saucer

that's all chipped!' she thought indignantly.

When she went to bed Eileen drew the curtain and looked out.

A few flakes of snow were falling – slowly, uncertainly, tumbling and dancing. They were piling up against the windows, the doors, the walls, the trees.

From her window Eileen could see the door of the shed. The little dark man peeped out, looked across at the room where he had seen the book, shook his head, and disappeared.

'I hope he'll be warm!' said Eileen anxiously.

She lay awake, planning to make friends with him. Wouldn't it be wonderful if he could tell where he came from, and all his adventures!

'If he isn't happy, of course I'll have to let him go back,' she thought mournfully as she fell asleep.

During the night she did not wake up once, yet she heard small, strong fingers trying to open the windows and the doors. Once Rose mee-owed crossly and twice Big Fella howled. In the stable Darkie stamped uneasily, but Long Ears wagged his ears, hee-hawed to himself and slept securely.

Eileen and Seamus were determined to keep every one of their New Year resolutions, but they had made so many that it wasn't going to be an easy year for them – that was sure!

'How can I talk nothing but Irish?' grumbled Seamus. 'I hardly know any.'

He had made that resolution to please his mother, but he was such a chatterbox that he couldn't remember a quarter of the Irish words he needed.

'I'll help you there,' his mother told him. 'I mustn't forget!'

'Dear! Dear!' sighed the turf-cutter. 'It's going to be terrible hard on an ignoramus like meself. Still, no doubt it'll be good for me.'

'I know which are going to be my hardest resolutions,' murmured Eileen as each day she had to find food for the little dark man without letting anyone in on her secret.

For she had made up her mind to start on no more adventures without telling the others.

She had also made up her mind that if she got into a scrape she would get out of it by herself.

Two very difficult resolutions for Eileen to keep!

She knew the little dark man would lead her into adventures. She knew that Seamus would be glad to share them.

The hardest thing of all was her dread that if she spoke of the dark stranger before she had to, he might be frightened into running away without a chance to get back where he belonged.

She didn't want harm to come to him.

She didn't want to part with him!

Eileen had such exciting games with her dolls that sometimes Seamus would join in, though he always declared that dolls were silly, babyish things, and he was surprised at Eileen bothering with them.

But Eileen never sat nursing her dolls. She scarcely ever made new clothes for them When the ones they had were worn out, she pinned gay pieces of stuff round them, turning a Dutch doll into a gipsy, and a sailor into a Red Indian or a pirate!

Seamus had made two bows, and when Eileen's dolls were stuck up in the grass it was great fun to stalk and shoot them.

Seamus had to promise never really to shoot the dolls.
'They might feel it! You can't be sure!' said Eileen.

She shot so carefully that her arrows never went near
the dolls!

'It gives them a chance to duck down or run,' she explained.

Seamus had made a pile of long straight arrows winged
with goose quills. He didn't want to ask Eileen to bring
out her dolls, and he began to feel cross with her for not
doing it without being asked.

Evening after evening he sat peeling the willow
wands he had gathered and binding the feathers tightly
with thin twine. He liked Eileen to help him with his
work, but she didn't seem to notice what he was doing at
all!

'It isn't fair!' thought Seamus indignantly. 'I haven't
quarrelled with her. I've waited for her every morning,
and I lent her my new pen yesterday when she had forgotten her own. I haven't done a thing to make her
sulky.'

He made so many arrows that he used up all the goose
feathers he could find, and still Eileen took no notice of
them!

Every evening Eileen came home from school and sat
with her story-book in her arms. She didn't read it. She
didn't even look at the pictures!

She didn't tie one end of her skipping-rope to the gate-
post and ask Seamus to turn. She had hardly bounced
her new ball, and her dolls, the old and the new, sat in a
row on top of the chest of drawers in her room, looking
very solemn and forlorn.

'I can't make out what ails the child,' said her mother
one day, when the turf-cutter was in the kitchen rubbing

goose fat into his boots.

'Sure she's looking grand. God bless her!' he replied, whistling softly as he worked. 'She always was a little dreamer. The darlin'!'

'It's that silly old story-book!' said Seamus scornfully. 'I know what I'll do! I'll hide it!'

When they set off for school the following morning, Seamus purposely left his spelling book behind.

They were within sight of the bridge when he pretended to discover its absence.

'You go on slowly,' he told Eileen. 'I'll race there and back.'

He rushed away and Eileen hopped first on one foot, then on the other, so that she would not hurry and could yet keep warm.

From where she waited she could see Seamus running into the cabin and out again.

'He found his book very quickly,' thought Eileen in wonder.

Seamus came back smiling. He was quite sure Eileen would never discover where he had hidden her story-book!

Seamus wasn't nearly so good as Eileen at keeping secrets. All the way home from school and while they were having tea, he had to keep stopping himself from asking Eileen where she had left her book, or was she going to read, or had she finished all the stories?

At last she got up from the table and went into her room to get the book!

Eileen was puzzled. She remembered putting the book there before she went to bed.

She came running into the kitchen.

'Mummie! Did you move my book?' she asked. 'The

new one that Aunt Kathleen gave me.'

'No, dear,' replied her mother, without looking up from the stocking she was darning.

She hadn't heard Seamus threaten to hide the book.

Eileen searched her room. She searched the whole cabin. She hunted high. She hunted low. But she could not find her book.

Seamus chuckled to himself. How clever he felt!

Then Eileen began to cry! She didn't make a noise, but she sat in the big armchair, hiding her face. Her shoulders shook and her handkerchief became a wet rag – that was all. But Seamus was upset. Eileen wasn't a cry-baby and he had expected her to get over her loss much more easily. 'If she is so very fond of her old book, I'll have to get it for her,' he thought. 'How could I know she'd be such a little duffer!'

Seamus went quickly out of the cabin. It was terribly dark in the garden and strange sounds were all round him and coming across the bog. There was scarcely any wind, and he could hear the twigs of trees and bushes rubbing against each other. There were scufflings and rustlings in the grass, and high in the air were faint cries as though birds were flying above the clouds.

Seamus wanted badly to go back into the warm bright house. He had come without putting on his coat and he was shivering. But he knew that if he returned for it he would not venture out again that night.

He couldn't bear to think of Eileen crying quietly to herself. He must get the book for her. After all, he wasn't afraid of the dark. There wasn't anything to be afraid of. The dark couldn't hurt him!

Seamus kept close to the wall of the house until he was opposite the old tool-shed. He could not see it in the darkness, but he knew exactly where it was.

He walked straight across to the door and thrust out his hand to push it open.

But the door was not closed! It stood wide open before him and yet Seamus hung back. He was afraid to enter!

He could hear no sound from the shed. Yet Seamus felt sure that something or someone was crouching there a few feet away.

It was all Seamus could do not to turn and run. How he wished he had never touched Eileen's book, for he had hidden it in the tool-shed and he would have to go and find it in that awful darkness.

He tried to be brave. He told himself that maybe Big Fella had got in there, or even Rose.

But Seamus was sure that if Rose or Big Fella had got into the shed he would soon know. Rose would purr even if she were too lazy to move, and he would see her green eyes gleaming in the darkness. While Big Fella would put his nose into his hand.

'Besides, they'd never keep so quiet,' thought Seamus.

He was trying to prevent himself running away, for as he came out of the kitchen he had seen Big Fella stretched before the fire with Rose lying on top of him.

'I'll just feel round for Eileen's book,' he decided, 'then I'll bolt! That's what I came for, and I don't care who's in here once I get the book.'

He put out one foot and took a step forward. He tried to move noiselessly, but his boots were new and thick and, in spite of all his efforts, they squeaked terribly.

Seamus held his breath. He was ready to jump backwards, but nothing happened.

Somehow his courage returned and he stepped boldly right into the shed.

A broken box filled with nails and screws stood on a shelf against the wall. It was in this Seamus had put Eileen's book. He reached out his hand and felt for it. His fingers touched nails and screws : nothing else !

There was no longer a book in the box !

Who had taken it ?

To make sure Seamus bent down and groped on the floor, but there was no trace of the book.

At the same moment he saw two points of light in the far corner !

Seamus was too scared to cry out. But already his eyes were growing used to the darkness, and he could make out a small man or a boy crouched there on a heap of hay.

He clenched his fists.

'Who are you?' he demanded hoarsely. 'What are you doing in our shed?'

There was no answer and Seamus took a step forward.

Suddenly he saw a big square book clasped in the trespasser's arms. It was the missing story-book !

Seamus was too angry to be frightened any longer.

'You thief !' he cried. 'Give me back that book !'

Seamus held out his hand, but the little dark man neither moved nor answered. Puzzled at his silence, Seamus strode across the shed and bent down to seize the book.

To his amazement the creature in the corner leaped over his head and sprang through the open door. As he went he gave Seamus a kick that sent him sprawling.

Up sprang Seamus and dashed out into the garden.

Down the snow-clad path went the little dark man, his leather bag on his back and Eileen's book under his arm.

The moon was high over the trees and the clouds were gone. The garden had been dark when Seamus first came out, but it was light now. The boy could see the strange figure running swiftly as a hare, and he knew that the fugitive was no tinker or wanderer of that countryside.

He was so glad to see the back of him that he forgot why he was there until he noticed Eileen's shadow on the window-blind.

'Stop thief!' shouted Seamus; but though he was a quick runner, he had delayed, and the little dark man had reached the gate and vaulted over it before Seamus had rounded the side of the cabin.

At his cry the turf-cutter flung open the door.

'Where are you, Seamus?' he called anxiously.

As the boy came in sight his father frowned.

'What game are you playing?' he asked sternly.

'A man has stolen Eileen's book,' replied Seamus. 'He has gone down the road.'

The turf-cutter looked puzzled.

'How in the wide world could he steal the child's book from the cabin?' he asked. ' 'Tis dreamin' ye are!'

Seamus tried to explain.

'I hid Eileen's book in the tool-shed because she was so silly about it. She wouldn't play or do anything but sit holding it. Then when she made such a fuss I went to get it for her. There was a little man in the shed and he had taken it. When I asked him for it he ran away.'

'Mebbe that will teach you not to be so clever another time!' exclaimed the turf-cutter indignantly. 'Isn't it fine that Eileen is to lose her book because of your nonsense!'

While they were speaking Eileen and her mother came to the door. The red glow from the fire and the white light from the lamp on the table streamed out across the snow.

There was the track of bare feet once more leading to
the gate.

Eileen's face was pale and tear-stained, but she was no
longer crying.

When she heard what had happened and saw that
the dark stranger had fled into the cold night she knew
she must give up her secret.

'It's all my fault,' she said. 'He came out of the book
the night daddy hurt his foot on the bog and I didn't
want him to go back. Now he'll be lost and cold and
hungry.'

She began to cry again.

'Whist now!' said the turf-cutter, patting Eileen on
the shoulder. 'Let's come in now and talk this over. At
the moment I'm not sure whether I'm on me head or
me heels.'

They went in to the fire and Eileen told her story. Then
Seamus told his.

The turf-cutter laughed.

'Don't fret, Eileen! 'Tis one of them lads of tinkers has
stolen yer book. I thought there might be some of them
prowling round, and I lying out on the bog. He'll know
how to take care of himself, never fear! But I'm afeard
you've seen the last of your story-book. Still, the next Fair
day we'll be over at the town and you shall have your
choice of a book.'

'And I'll put some food and a blanket in the shed in
case he comes back,' said her mother kindly. 'He may be
a queer chap, and he's surely very poor to be going barefoot in this hard weather. Maybe I could let him have
some clothes of Seamus's if he comes this way again.'

But Eileen was quite sure he would not come back!

Seamus knew he was to blame for the loss of the book

and he tried to comfort his sister.

'The dark man has the book, so if he wants to go back into it he can,' he told her. 'I am sorry I lost it for you, and I'm thinking of something to make up for it. But you'd sooner the little chap had it, wouldn't you, now?'

Eileen nodded mournfully.

'I would, indeed!' she replied.

But she watched the marks of bare feet in the snow until the falling flakes covered them up.

There was always great excitement on Fair day, and this time Eileen jumped out of bed without waiting to be called. She loved reading stories and she was to have a new book! She still grieved about the one she had lost and the vanished stranger, but she wondered what book she would bring home with her.

'Get a book with pictures,' suggested Seamus.

'One with pieces of poetry would be grand,' said her father.

'Sure the child can't choose until she sees them,' laughed her mother.

Even Long Ears and Darkie seemed to know that this wasn't an ordinary Fair day, and Rose came as far as the gate to see them off.

'There'll be rain soon!' declared the turf-cutter as they crossed the bridge and saw the water-rat sitting on the bank, smoothing his whiskers!

He stared after them, then plunged into the water and swam quickly, as if he were trying to keep up with them.

20

The little dark man

ll the people on the road to
the Fair kept glancing anxiously up at the sky, hoping
to finish their buying and
selling before the weather broke.

Eileen and Seamus sat up behind Darkie, feeling very
proud of their new leather coats with sou'westers to match.
They loved the snow, but they almost wished it would
rain, to prove what fine clothes they were wearing.

They even had big rubber boots up to their knees, and
all this grandeur was a present from Aunt Una in Kerry!

'I'll write and tell her about my story-book and the
little dark man,' said Eileen. 'Aunt Una would believe
what I told her. I know she would.'

She hadn't much more time for talking, for there was
the town and there was the Fair!

And at that moment down came the rain, washing
away the piled-up snow, filling the gutters, flooding the
roads, swelling the streams, and gliding down the smooth
leather coats worn by Eileen and Seamus.

Eileen's coat was green, so that now she seemed dressed
in seaweed. But Seamus was in brown and he hoped he
looked like a fisherman.

'I don't wonder the water-rat looked happy,' he said.
'He'd be sure to like this weather.'

'But he wouldn't like a flood, would he?' asked Eileen.
'I should hate him to be flooded out.'

Before Seamus could answer their progress was stopped
by a huge crowd waiting to get into a tent.

'Do let's go into a show!' cried Eileen. 'I'd love to see
a lion or a tiger.'

'You can amuse yourselves for a couple of hours,' the
turf-cutter told the children. 'Don't get into mischief and
meet us under the clock when it strikes twelve.'

He went off leading Long Ears and Darkie, while
Eileen and Seamus, shaking the rain from their leather
coats, joined the throng squeezing into the tent.

As they paid out their money a school friend of Seamus
got in front of them.

'It isn't a wild animal,' he said. 'It's a savage. They
captured him in the jungle. He's dressed in skins, and
he eats raw meat and swallows lighted candles whole!'

'I don't think I want to see him!' exclaimed Eileen,
drawing back.

'Don't believe a word you say! So there, Micky
Reardon!' declared Seamus scornfully.

'You never believe anything,' complained Micky.
'Look here! I'll bet you my electric torch against your
knife that it is a savage.'

'Your torch doesn't light up!' objected Seamus.

'Well – your knife is broken.'

'Move on there!' shouted the man who was taking
the money.

Seamus clutched Eileen's arm. A push and a squeeze
and there they were inside the big tent!

'Don't forget!' said Micky. 'My torch against your

knife!'

Seamus did not hear him. The shouting of the showman up near the platform, the chatter and laughter, the scuffling of feet and the cries of those who could not see, made such an uproar that he was deafened.

At first they could see very little. The tent was closely packed. On most Fair days the show tents were empty until the evening, but the heavy rain was driving people in to shelter wherever they could.

Eileen and Seamus were surrounded by people nearly twice as tall as themselves, and Eileen was wishing she had stayed outside when Seamus grabbed her arm.

'Get up on my shoulder!' he said. 'One of us had better see something.'

'I'm too heavy,' she objected.

Seamus took no notice of that and, using his arm as a step, she scrambled to his shoulder.

It was a very unsteady seat, for the crowd pushed and swayed, and for a moment she was so confused she didn't know which way to look.

At last she saw the platform. A row of tin oil-lamps had been put along the front. Beyond them was a pail filled with glowing sods. Crouched beside it, chipping spearheads from a pile of flints as fast as he could, was a little dark man, dressed in skins and looking very strange and puzzled.

The showman was selling the spearheads at threepence each, and all the time he shouted at the top of his voice:

'This is the only one left of the tribe. He was captured in the African jungle after a terrible hand-to-hand struggle. Doesn't know a word of any language. He eats raw meat and drinks melted tallow. Buy one of these spearheads as a memento. All the work of his own unaided hands. Now then, ladies and gents, money first. Then pass quietly out and give someone else a chance!'

No one passed out. They all wanted to see the little dark man eat raw meat.

Another showman stepped out on the platform from the back. He carried a plate with several bits of raw meat on it, which he handed to the little man crouching by the fire.

The little man shook his head and pushed the plate away, but it was thrust back, and the other showman stuck his head over the footlights and looked so threatening that the poor little fellow picked up the smallest bit of raw meat and began to nibble it. He made such faces that everyone could tell he hated the horrid stuff, and several people said it was a shame and oughtn't to be allowed.

Eileen was staring in amazement. She had forgotten all about Seamus, who decided he couldn't hold her up any longer, and down she came with a thump.

'What's he like?' he asked. 'I do wish I could see a bit. It isn't fair. And I shall have to give Micky Reardon my knife.'

'Indeed you won't!' cried Eileen. 'The poor little thing isn't a savage at all! He's our little dark man. He does look so unhappy. They're making him eat raw meat and he hates it. You can see he does. Oh, Seamus! What shall we do? We can't go out and leave him here!'

Seamus was standing on tiptoe, hopping on one leg and trying his hardest to get a glimpse of the platform. But it was all no use. All the tall men and women in the countryside seemed to have come into the tent.

'We'll have to rescue him,' he told Eileen. 'But first we must get nearer. Push hard!'

Eileen wasn't good at pushing, but she did her best. Luckily some of the people were going out and that left a little more room.

Wriggling and squeezing, Eileen tried to follow Seamus.

How hot and stifling it was! She stopped to draw a deep breath, and at once a big farmer stepped in front of her. When she wriggled round him Seamus was out of sight. Eileen tried to force her way in the direction she hoped he had taken. But it was hard work.

She could not move another inch. A stout market woman blocked the way.

Eileen tried to wriggle round her and discovered that the woman was carrying a huge basket. It was easy to duck under this, and when she came up at the other side Eileen found herself jammed against the platform right at the side of the tent.

She could not see Seamus. The little dark man was mournfully gazing at his raw meat and the showman was shouting that the show was over :

'Pass along, ladies and gents! Pass along! Next house, please! Pass along!'

He was pushing the people out into the rain. If they wanted to come back they must pay another threepence. But out they had to go!

'If I go out I won't be able to come back,' thought Eileen. 'Even twopence half-price for children is a terrible lot of money when you haven't got it.'

She looked at the little dark man. His back was turned to her. He was carefully examining the last spearhead he had made.

Eileen wondered how she could attract his attention without the showman seeing her.

'If only I could find Seamus!' she thought anxiously. Suddenly the little dark man stood up, swung his hand and let fly. The spearhead struck the showman on the back of the head!

Luckily he had a thick mat of carroty hair, but the sharp point of the spearhead gave him such a jab that he let out a roar of anger and pain. This so terrified the people that they struggled and fought to get out of the tent.

The little dark man danced up and down, rubbed and slapped his hands, and grinned with delight.

Eileen clambered on to the platform and ran over to him.

He stared at her, then smiled. She took him by the hand and pulled him to the edge of the platform. He went willingly. Jumping down they got underneath and, as Eileen had hoped, they were able to creep from under the tent into the open air.

They came out at the side farthest from the entrance.

The rain had stopped. A bitter wind blew down from the mountain. At a distance there were crowds of people. But all those who had heard the roars of the showman were gathered at the entrance of the tent. Once more Eileen longed for Seamus. But she had to do her best without him.

'We must get away before anyone sees us,' thought Eileen.

The little dark man talked rapidly to her, then smiled. He was happy to be with her, and Eileen was delighted with his friendliness. She wished she could understand him, but there was no time to bother about that now.

If they could hide somewhere until twelve o'clock, or if she could disguise the little dark man!

That wouldn't be easy!

Eileen wondered if they could make a dash through the Fair to where the carts were waiting and hide in one. But she was terrified that the little dark man might be caught and taken back.

As they stood hand in hand behind a pile of empty boxes, such a splendid idea came into Eileen's mind that she laughed for joy.

'What a duffer I am not to have thought of it before!' she exclaimed.

She took off her sou'wester and slipped it on the little man's head.

It almost hid his face and Eileen began to feel excited.

Next she unfastened her leather coat and coaxed him into it. She was perished without it, but that didn't matter.

The little dark man was so small that she managed to button the coat up to his chin and buckle the belt, though it was a tight fit!

He was still barefoot, but who would notice that?

He was so pleased with himself that he pranced up and down, but Eileen scolded him so firmly that though he couldn't understand a word she said, he knew she wanted him to keep quiet.

Taking his hand in hers, she led him out into the market-place.

Eileen wanted to run, but she knew they would be safer if they walked quietly. She had been glad that there were no people near them, but it made her feel that the women at the stalls and the farmers with their cattle were watching her and her companion as they approached.

The little dark man splashed through the puddles and peeped out from under his hat, as though they were doing it for fun. When they came to the first stall Eileen was so glad that she forgot her caution and let go his hand.

Eileen had never seen this stall before. A man was washing potatoes in a bucket of water and putting them into a chopper which cut them into strips. He tipped the strips into a huge frying-pan of boiling fat, and when they were cooked lifted them out in a wire basket.

They were piled up crisp and golden. As fast as the man could cook the people bought.

'Come along!' he shouted. 'The only chips at the Fair and the best in all Ireland! Twopence a bag! Twopence a bag!'

It was a long time since breakfast. Eileen felt in her pocket. She had two pennies left.

The little dark man sniffed. He thought it a lovely smell. A woman taking a bag of chips from the man dropped one. The little man picked it up and poked it into his mouth.

Never had he tasted anything like it! He much preferred chips to raw meat! Reaching out; he grabbed two handfuls from the pile in front of the stall!

The chip-potato man couldn't believe his eyes. It wasn't only the theft which amazed him, but beneath the damp sou'wester he had seen, instead of a child's face – a bearded man's!

He dropped the scoop he was using to measure out the chips.

'Hand them back! Ye impident thief, ye!' he shouted.

Gobbling the chips as he ran, the little dark man rushed away.

He couldn't understand one word, but he could read an angry face.

'The greedy little creature!' thought Eileen angrily. 'Why couldn't he wait?'

She flung her pennies down on the stall.

'That's to pay for the chips!' she cried, and started in pursuit.

Unluckily the little dark man, instead of dodging among the stalls, fled across the open space back towards the tents.

The showman, a handkerchief tied about his wounded head, was coming out of the big tent. The people crowding round him were saying what a terrible thing it was that a murderous savage should be running loose through the town!

Seamus, looking in vain for Eileen, heard what they were saying and felt very worried.

He feared to go away from the tent, for that was where he had last seen his sister. But he was sure that she had got away with the little dark man.

'I do wish I knew where to look for her,' he muttered gloomily, when a hand gripped his arm.

'Hand over that knife!' ordered Micky Reardon. 'Didn't I tell you he was a savage dressed in skins and that he ate raw meat?'

'Well, he never swallowed a lighted candle,' complained Seamus.

'That's because you only went in once!' declared Micky. 'The first time he ate raw meat. The second time he'll swallow a lighted candle. You see!'

He held out his hand for the knife. He had envied Seamus because of it since the day it appeared in school. Micky wanted to carve his name on desks and doors!

Seamus took out his knife and looked at it. He liked it more than any knife he had seen. It had four blades, a corkscrew, a hook of getting stones out of horse's hooves, and in the back was a file. Two of the blades were broken and one was a bit jagged, while the corkscrew was blunt and the hook had been worn straight, but the file was almost as good as new!

Seamus felt he couldn't bear to part with it.

'I'll give it up when I've seen the savage swallow a lighted candle!' he said firmly.

'That's not fair!' cried Micky. 'He's run away. You know he has!'

Before Seamus could answer they heard a shout and saw Eileen, bare-headed and without a coat, running after someone who was wearing her leather coat and her sou'wester.

At once both boys thought they had been stolen from her. Even Seamus did not recognize the little dark man.

'Come on!' shouted Micky. 'We'll get them back for her! Stop thief! Stop thief!'

He liked Eileen, because, when she had won an enormous sugar walking-stick at the Fair she had given him a big lump.

The boys raced towards Eileen. The little dark man saw them coming. He saw, too, his enemy the showman. He had eaten all the chips. He wanted more. He decided to go back to the stall. He turned suddenly and crashed into Eileen. Over she went – the little dark man on top of her!

'You help Eileen! I'll hold the thief!' screamed Micky.

Eileen knew there was no time to explain to Seamus. She was bruised and shaken, but she was determined to save the little dark man. They scrambled up together, but Eileen held his hand tightly and pulled him away from the tents, away from the stalls towards the quays.

'We can hide among the sheds!' she decided. 'When they've given up looking for us we'll go round the back of the town and meet mummy and daddy.'

'Eileen!' called Seamus. 'Eileen! Don't run! It's me and Micky!'

He was puzzled, so was Micky. They couldn't understand why Eileen was running hand in hand with the thief.

Eileen looked back. She wanted Seamus to know what she was doing, but the showman was following, for he was very curious and he wanted to vent his temper on someone.

The little dark man looked back too. The edge of the big cap caught in the collar of the coat and tumbled off. A cry went up as his dark bushy head was seen.

'Let me get me hands on him!' roared the showman, racing across the green.

He was a big man with long legs. He rushed by Seamus and Micky, and Eileen trembled as she heard his feet pounding on the ground.

The little man was a wonderful runner. He could easily have escaped, but he would not abandon Eileen. She ran her hardest, thinking she was saving him; but he had to slow down to let her keep up with him.

Her breath came in gasps. She couldn't go another step. What were they to do?

The canal was in front of them. Big cakes of ice floated on the surface. A barge was tied to a post, but the quay was deserted. Every one was at the Fair.

'If we can only get time to hide, we'll escape,' thought Eileen hopefully.

But, as she staggered on to the cobblestones the showman was barely a dozen yards behind!

On went the little man, turning neither to the right nor to the left; and now he was dragging Eileen.

She thought she knew what he meant to do – jump into the water and swim to the other side!

Eileen loved swimming, but in the clean sea on a hot day, not in a dirty half-frozen canal!

Seamus saw what was happening and cried out in horror.

'Stop!' he shouted at the showman. 'If you hurt my sister, I'll –'

Seamus did not finish his threat. He saw Eileen and the little dark man reach the edge of the quay. He saw them jump. But he heard no splash, and when he and Micky caught up to the showman, who was standing as if turned to stone, he could see no sign of anyone in the water.

'I bet they're hiding on the barge!' declared Micky Reardon.

They ran in a crowd to the barge. It was loaded with turf, but they searched every bit of it and could not find a trace of the fugitives.

The showman looked so unhappy that even Seamus couldn't say a word to him.

'I know I was to blame,' he said. 'But I give my solemn word I never meant to hurt a hair of the child's head. I won't go back to me show till I find her!'

21
Through the book

ileen and the little dark man were not hiding on the barge. They were not in the canal. Where were they? As th ey reached the edge of the quay Eileen saw that the water-rat was sitting on one of the pieces of ice. His little bright eyes watched her. His ears stood up. His whiskers waved. His tail twitched.

Beside him lay a wet, tattered book. He opened it, and as they jumped Eileen saw the picture of a forest. The next moment she fell into a thick dry bed of moss and rolled over and over.

As last she lay still. She kept her eyes shut, for though she wasn't hurt she was frightened. A gentle hand stroked her hair. She opened her eyes and there was the little dark man sitting beside her.

He was smiling at her, and when he spoke she understood him.

'Don't be afraid!' he said. 'Back there you were good to me. Here I'll take care of you.'

'Where are we?' she asked.

'In the great forest!' he replied.

Eileen looked about her. There were tall trees stretch-

212

ing on every side. Overhead they were so thick that the light was faint and green. She could hear no sound but the branches swaying and the trickling of a hidden stream.

'Where is Seamus?' asked Eileen.

'Back there,' the little man told her.

'Can I go to him?' Eileen wanted to know.

'When the time comes we will find the road. Until then you must stay here!'

Eileen stood up. The little dark man anxiously watched her face. She wished she had Seamus with her, though she didn't feel in the least bit afraid, and she was determined to make the most of her time and see all she could.

'First I'll explore the forest,' she thought to herself.

She had become used to taking care of the little man and now turned to take his hand. To her surprise he pulled off the leather coat and tucked it neatly between the roots of a giant beech. From the hollow beneath another root he drew out a heavy iron spear and shield, and he smiled proudly when he saw how astonished she was.

'Keep with me,' he said. 'Don't stray and you'll be safe.'

'Shall I bring my coat?' asked Eileen. 'Someone might take it while we're away.'

The little dark man broke off a green bough from the beech and laid it on the coat.

'That is my mark!' he told her. 'For I am Sreng of the Beeches, and there is not one who will touch that coat. Keep close now!'

He started off among the trees and Eileen would soon have been left behind, only he kept stopping to beat his shield with his spear.

One! Two! Three! Four! He kept to this time, so that it sounded like a march played on a drum.

At last there came an answering drumming and shouts of welcome.

'Listen to what I shall say and do not contradict me!' Sreng warned her. 'We have come at a time of great danger and you must be very wise.'

'I won't say a word,' promised Eileen.

As they hurried along another sound came to them – the sound of rushing water, and Eileen saw the sunlight dancing upon tossing waves.

They came suddenly upon a clearing among the trees. A fire burnéd in the centre and around it had been built a circle of wooden huts. From these many small dark people rushed to meet Sreng, but when they saw Eileen they stopped and raised their spears, while they peered at her from behind their shields.

But a man taller than the rest stepped forward without shield or spear. Eileen could tell that he was the only one there, except Sreng, who did not fear her.

'Is this maiden a prisoner you have captured, O Sreng?' he asked.

Sreng of the Beeches shook his head.

'This child befriended me when I went among the strangers,' he said. 'She has come among us as a messenger. Let us take great care of her, or we shall be destroyed!'

The men dropped their spears. The women who had caught up their babies put them down on the grass again and the chief bowed to Eileen.

'What is your message?' he asked. 'Do your people come as friends or as enemies?'

Eileen was puzzled. But she tried to answer wisely.

'I am your friend,' she replied. 'You see, we all belong here just as you do, only we live in a different time.'

The little dark men didn't know what to make of that,

but Sreng persuaded them to let Eileen rest and to give her some food while he told his story.

They made her sit on a heap of dried leaves and brought her flat sweet cakes and a horn of honey and water.

Sreng of the Beeches sat on the ground. The chief sat on a carved wooden stool and the rest of the people stood round.

'These strangers who came in a cloud,' said Sreng, 'are far richer and braver than we are. They can build houses of stone. Their weapons are small and light. A spear only half as long and thick as mine will travel twice as far, and instead of stone heads they are tipped with metal. The strangers are tall and fair and have great knowledge of magic. The clothes even of the poorest among them are embroidered with coloured threads and shine with gold and precious stones. They have brought many treasures with them – an invincible sword, a magic spear, and a cauldron which will feed a host of fighting men without needing to be refilled. Yet they are friendly and are willing to share with us.'

'We will fight them and have all these treasures for ourselves!' said the chief, and there was great applause for his words.

'Why should we fight them?' asked Sreng. 'They are exiles just as we once were. They offer to take the land we do not need. They will teach us to live better and more happily. They do not quarrel among themselves as we do. But they make music, sing, dance, and tell stories.'

'What name is on them?' asked the chief.

'They call themselves the Danaans,' replied Sreng. 'And if we are wise we shall accept their friendship.'

But the chief was greedy, so were the others. They

began to quarrel over the division of the treasures they were sure they would win from the Danaans. When they began to fight, Sreng caught up his spear and sprang into the middle of the struggle.

Not one of them would stand up to him. It was easy to see he was the bravest of them all.

'You have not seen their weapons!' cried Sreng angrily. 'Yet you speak of fighting them. Wait! I will show you!'

He called one of the boys to him and sent him off through the forest. In a few moments the boy returned, carrying a gleaming spear and a gaily decorated shield. They were so light that a child could carry them, but when Sreng flung the spear at the strongest shield they had, the blade went right through.

The chief lifted his spear and flung it at the Danaan shield, but it fell to the ground bent and twisted, while the shield wasn't even dented!

The dark, little people were amazed, but still they did not want to make friends with the wonderful strangers. They wanted to defeat them and loot their treasures.

Sreng and the chief sat arguing. The people of the forest grew tired of listening. Some lay down to sleep, others drank and ate, while the children played and swam or went fishing in light leather boats.

A boy with a thick fuzzy mop of hair picked up one of the boats which was lying on the bank and marched down to the water, carrying it on his head. Eileen ran after him.

'Let me come too!' she called eagerly.

The boy frowned, but Sreng was watching and he nodded sulkily.

Eileen stepped carefully into the boat, which bobbed up and down like a balloon.

'What is it made of?' she asked curiously.

'Sreng says our ancestors made these boats from the leather bags they brought with them when they came from over the sea,' replied the boy. 'They are very, very old. But they are the best boats in the whole world.'

Fuzzy, as Eileen called him in her mind, bragged on. He said he was the fastest swimmer, the best boatman, the cleverest fisher of all the boys in the tribe.

'Can you dive?' asked Eileen scornfully.

Fuzzy shivered. No! He didn't like jumping into the water upside down.

'You should see my brother dive!' Eileen told him. 'He can do a back dive, a double dive, and a swallow dive!'

'He must have good magic,' said Fuzzy, looking very annoyed.

Eileen shrugged her shoulders.

'It isn't magic at all. He's just clever and he never brags about it either.'

Fuzzy scowled, but he showed her how to keep the boat straight so that it climbed each wave easily and without shipping any water, while he fished from the other end.

Soon the boat was half filled with gleaming, shivering fish and then he pulled in a huge salmon! No doubt about it, Fuzzy was a clever fisherman!

The salmon leaped frantically, trying to get over the side of the boat into the river again. Fuzzy looked about him for a block of wood to strike down the great fish. For a moment his back was turned. The salmon lifted its big head and looked appealingly at Eileen.

It made a queer noise and flapped its tail, and she was sure it said in a gasp:

'Help me out! Help me out!'

Eileen put her hands under the salmon and tipped it back into the water!

Fuzzy glanced round and saw what she had done!

Never had he seen such an enormous salmon! He had caught it so easily and there it was swimming away, shaking its tail as if mocking him.

A fishing spear lay in the bottom of the boat. He picked it up, determined to teach this interfering stranger to mind her own business.

Eileen saw his furious face and guessed what he was going to do with the spear. She wanted to cover her eyes and scream, but that wouldn't be much good. She heard a shout from the bank. It was Sreng, warning Fuzzy not to touch her, but Eileen was too scared to know that. With a cry of terror she backed away, slipped on the squirming fish, and toppled over into the rushing river!

For a moment she was too startled to strike out. She kept her mouth shut as she went down, but as she came up and her face lifted above water, she drew a deep breath and began to swim.

The current was strong, the river wide, and Eileen knew she had little chance of reaching the bank. Besides, she was too frightened to want to return there. Sreng was her friend, but the others were so quarrelsome she did not want to see them again.

The river was full of rocks, and she had to watch out to prevent herself being dashed against them. The spray fell in showers on her face, her head began to swim, and her eyes half closed.

'If I'm carried right out to sea I shall never get back,' she thought sadly.

A cross current seized her and whirled her round. Gasping and helpless, she tried to cling to a rock, but she was dragged away by the force of the river.

Suddenly something smooth and swift rose under her, and she was lifted above the fury of the stream.

Eileen shook her head and blinked hard. To her surprise she was still being carried down the stream, but the waves no longer dashed over her, and as she came near a rock she was swept to one side and passed without touching it.

At last she looked down and nearly tumbled into the river again, for she was seated on the back of a huge salmon – the salmon she had helped out of the boat!

'Oh!' said Eileen. 'I wonder what will happen next!'

She soon found out.

At one point the bank sloped gently down to a sandy cove, and as they reached this the salmon swam close in and stopped.

Eileen stepped ashore.

'Thank you,' she said. 'Thank you, very much. I'll never eat salmon again.'

The great silvery fish turned red with anger and lashed the water with his tail.

'Oh! I am sorry,' faltered Eileen. 'I didn't think how awful it must sound to you. I am very grateful. I did not mean to be rude.'

The salmon grew silver once more.

'I am not angry with you,' he replied in his queer gasping voice. 'I am too wise for that, and yet I am surprised that one who has ridden on the Salmon of Wisdom should be so foolish.'

With a flick of his tail he swam away, while Eileen flushed with shame.

'I'll have to try really hard to get wise,' she told herself. 'It would be so useful. And yet all the salmon's wisdom didn't save him from being caught!'

As Eileen stood watching the salmon she heard a chorus of shouts from higher up the river. Fuzzy was paddling downstream at a great rate. Two boats crowded with yelling boys followed, while on the bank, several men with Sreng of the Beeches far in advance rushed wildly along.

They were on the other bank, but Eileen knew they were after her. She trusted Sreng, but Fuzzy was coming nearer and nearer.

He was watching her so closely that he failed to see a rock which stuck up right in his way!

His leather boat caught on it, tipped up, swung round, turned upside down and, with a shower of wriggling fish falling on top of him, Fuzzy plunged into the river.

The boys in the other two boats stopped paddling to stare after their leader. They made no attempt to help him. Some laughed and jeered, others waved their arms and made faces.

'The mean things!' exclaimed Eileen indignantly. 'They might try to pull him out!'

But Fuzzy was in no danger, for he could swim like a fish, and the jeering boys were so occupied watching him that they took no notice of what was happening to themselves.

Suddenly the two boats were caught in a current and flung together. The paddles dropped overboard and the boats swung round and round!

There were the boys at the mercy of the raging river, but instead of being frightened they jumped out. Some went after the paddles. The others clung to the boats and, kicking their hardest, pushed them towards the bank.

The boys swam so well that Eileen forgot how wet she

was. But, when they all reached the bank, instead of getting once more into the boats and paddling, they turned these upside down on the bank and started running.

'They're getting dry!' thought Eileen, shivering a little.

They had covered half the distance between Eileen and the boats when one of the boys, without stopping, raised his hand and flung a small spear.

Eileen jumped just as it whizzed by her head. She didn't wait another moment, but ran!

A shower of spears followed her. How frightened she was, and how angry! But Eileen was nearly as good a runner as Seamus and, fast runners though these boys were, there wasn't one who could have beaten him.

Eileen looked over her shoulder to see if they were gaining on her. She trod on a smooth stone, slipped and fell.

'They'll get me now!' she thought.

But a great shout came across the river: 'STOP!'

It was Sreng's voice.

The boys stopped – all but Fuzzy, who had landed lower down and was running after her alone.

His hair was so plastered over his ears he did not hear the warning voice, and he was determined to punish Eileen.

She stumbled to her feet and faced him.

'I'm not going to run from one boy and he smaller than I am!' she thought indignantly.

Desperately Eileen caught up a sharp stone. But she did hate fighting.

'If only he'd let me explain,' she thought.

On came Fuzzy. He looked so ferocious that Eileen trembled. He was scarcely a dozen yards away when he stopped, turned a queer white and, with a cry of terror, spun on his heel and fled.

Eileen stared after him. What could have frightened Fuzzy?

A voice called her: 'Eileen! Eileen!'

She started, and turning with a glad cry, saw Seamus coming towards her.

Instead of running to meet him she rubbed her eyes. 'I'm asleep and dreaming, for sure!' she told herself.

She was standing near the gate of a walled city. The wall was of grey, gleaming stone, the gate of wrought bronze, and inside were wonderful streets and houses.

Seamus smiled and held out his hands to her. Eileen remained standing, for this was a Seamus she had never seen before.

He was dressed in a silk embroidered tunic. On his left arm was a gaily decorated shield like the one Sreng of the Beeches had shown the small dark people, and in his right hand he carried a slender spear which gleamed in the sunlight.

He had almost reached his sister before she noticed that his thick hair was bound with a gold circlet, studded with shining stones.

Where in the wide world did Seamus get so much grandeur? she wondered.

And look at the fuss he always made about putting on his Sunday clothes!

'Don't be frightened, Eileen,' he said. 'No one can hurt you now.'

Eileen went slowly towards Seamus. He looked splendid, and she was so dirty and tattered that she felt ashamed.

Suddenly he dropped his spear and shield and, running up to her, gave her a hug.

'Aren't you the plucky girl!' he cried. 'To jump

through that book and land here! But I am glad I've found you. I was beginning to get scared.'

'How did you find out where I'd gone?' asked Eileen curiously.

Seamus picked up his spear and leaned on it.

'When we couldn't find you and that little dark chap anywhere,' he said, 'I guessed something queer had happened. Then I saw the water-rat sitting up on the ice, holding your story-book. He had it open at the picture of the forest. There was a big hole torn in it as if someone had jumped right through. I knew then what you had done. I jumped too, but instead of finding myself in the frozen canal or the forest, I came here – in the city of the Danaans!'

'Oh!' said Eileen, looking at the city with its turrets and domes rising into the clear blue sky.

'You were with the Firbolgs,' Seamus told her. 'And I should think you're mighty glad to get away from them.'

'I would be,' replied Eileen, 'only for Sreng.'

'Sreng?' repeated Seamus. 'Who is he?'

Eileen told him her adventures.

As she finished, a man standing on the wall blew a silver trumpet.

'That means we must go inside,' said Seamus. 'They expect the Firbolgs to attack after dark.'

Eileen hung back.

'I can't go like this!' she protested. 'They'd all think I've been rolling in the dirt!'

Seamus laughed.

'They know all about you. And, you'd better not get stuck-up about it, but they think you're great. You see, I've told them you can sing and you know poetry. They're crazy about music and singing and things like that. And they're the friendliest, kindest people I've ever met. They'll rig you up in no time, just as they did me. Come along!'

Seamus pulled her towards the city. The sentinels were closing the gates, but they flung them wide open.

'Welcome, young wanderer!' they said, saluting Eileen.

She saluted in return. The silver gates clanged behind them and there she stood, hand in hand with Seamus in the main street of the magic city.

The road was wide and paved with white marble. On each side were planted fruit trees and wind-bells tinkled among their leaves. The houses stood back in gardens, each one different and each the loveliest Eileen could imagine. The windows were wide open and a buzz of music and laughter floated out.

Eileen could see people eating and drinking and she looked wistfully at Seamus.

'I am so hungry!' she told him. 'I do believe I'm almost starving!'

'You must be properly dressed first!' declared Seamus. 'You can't possibly eat while you're dirty!'

Eileen looked at Seamus in amazement. She couldn't get used to such particular ways. He flushed, but laughed and twirled his spear.

'You see, Eileen, everything is so clean and lovely here that it makes you feel strange if you're dirty and untidy.'

Eileen nodded and sighed. Before she could answer, her brother caught her by the arm and drew her back against the steps of a house as a procession swung round the corner.

It was headed by a tall man dressed like Seamus, only far grander, and on his head he wore a silver helmet with wings at the sides.

Behind him came many men, running and carrying on their shoulders an enormous cauldron from which rose a cloud of steam and all the lovely smells Eileen could think of.

They put down the cauldron at the steps of a house and out came a laughing crowd armed with dishes and spoons. They dipped into the cauldron and Eileen saw that each spoon brought out something different – roast meat, boiled meat, grilled meat, fish, sweets, fruit, pudding.

'Let's follow it!' urged Eileen eagerly.

'No need!' declared Seamus. 'When it has been through the city they will take it to the banqueting hall. Soldiers, dancers, singers, all the people who don't keep house, and strangers, will meet there.'

'It will be empty by then!' sighed Eileen.

Seamus shook his head.

'It will be as full at the end as it is now. It is the Cauldron of the Dagda!'

The procession moved on. Behind the cauldron marched a black elephant with twinkling eyes. Eileen clutched her brother's hand.

'Seamus! That's my elephant. I know it is!'

'Sh!' whispered Seamus. 'Don't be silly. How could it be? Yours is on the mantelpiece at home.'

Behind the elephant pranced a lovely white creature shaped like a deer, with one silver horn jutting from the centre of its forehead.

'The Unicorn!' said Seamus. 'You must bow to the Unicorn!'

They both bowed and the Unicorn tapped the ground with its silver horn.

There were tall shaggy wolf-hounds, riderless grey

horses with flowing manes and tails, elegant striped cats and snow-white leopards. Last of all marched a small, shaggy man with a long beard twisted into a plait and tied at the end with a golden cord. He was dressed in soft brown leather, and beside him trotted a dainty little white pig.

'There's the leprechaun!' cried Eileen. 'I'd know him anywhere!'

She was so delighted to see him that she danced up and down.

'I do wish you'd mind your manners!' scolded Seamus. 'You mustn't go shouting and screaming here! Of course it isn't the leprechaun. Danaans don't know there are such people!'

But Eileen was obstinate.

'It is him!' she declared. 'I'd know him anywhere!'

As the small man passed he put his finger to his nose and shut one eye, while the white pig flapped its ears and grunted.

'Let's go with him!' cried Eileen. 'Oh Seamus, do come!'

'We mustn't,' replied Seamus. 'But you'll see him again. He'll be at the feast.'

They went on under the trees. Eileen saw a golden yellow pear hanging within reach. She pulled it down, and when she put her teeth into it the juice spurted out.

'Wish we had a pear tree like that at home!' she thought.

They came to a pool with wide steps leading down to it.

'Walk through the water,' Seamus told Eileen. 'I'll meet you on the other side.'

Eileen walked slowly down the steps. The water was

deep blue and surged up to meet her. It was warm and scented, and she went in easily up to her neck.

When she came out at the other side her torn muddy frock had changed to a white silk tunic. Her thick leather shoes were soft white sandals and she felt fresh and strong.

A woman walked out from among the trees and smoothed Eileen's hair with a golden comb.

'Are you the little singer?' she asked. 'Go quickly now, for the feast is about to begin.'

As they ran through the wide streets they heard the guards on the walls blowing their silver trumpets.

'I do hope I'll be in the fight!' cried Seamus.

Eileen had forgotten all about the Firbolgs. Now she felt anxious for Sreng.

Following Seamus she came to a great hall with wide-open doors at each end. It was so lofty that the roof rose above the trees and the flags and banners hung from the rafters looked dim and small.

Down the centre of the hall was ranged a table with seats on each side. Already these were crowded and Eileen drew back shyly.

Inside the door stood the leprechaun, and he hailed her.

'Make way for the little wanderer with the golden voice!' he cried. Taking Eileen by the hand, he led her to the top of the table.

A tall man wearing a jewelled crown sat there. He smiled at Eileen.

'You are a brave child,' he said, 'and you are very welcome. How did you come here?'

Eileen was telling him when the great cauldron was placed on the table in front of her.

'Say what you want and take it out!' the tall man told her.

'White pudding and tomatoes!' was all she could think of.

But it was such lovely white pudding and so beautifully cooked that she didn't regret her choice a bit.

The next time she asked for strawberry ice-cream, and out it came!

'You know many strange things,' said the tall man. 'A frozen pudding is grand eating on a hot day!'

And in next to no time everyone at that Danaan feast was eating strawberry ice-cream!

'Isn't it queer!' said Seamus to the leprechaun, who was sitting beside him. 'Eileen does the queerest things and they turn out right!'

The moment everyone had eaten enough the cauldron was carried away, still steaming and sizzling.

'Now you must sing!' said the tall man to Eileen, leaning back in his seat and smiling at her.

Behind her was a young man holding a harp on his knee. He waited for her to begin, and through her song she could hear his music running after her voice and creeping up behind.

She was very shy, but she began at once: *The Snowy-Breasted Pearl.*

Eileen could never sing that without the tears coming into her eyes, and when she had finished everyone in the hall was weeping for the dead girl in the song.

'Maybe I should sing a fighting song,' she said to the tall man. 'I'd sing a happy one, only I just can't remember one at the moment. But there's one about the Irish Brigade.'

'It would give me great pleasure to hear that song,'

replied the tall man.

So she sang them, 'The mess tent is full and the glasses are set.'

As she sang the last line and the young man gave a glorious flourish across his strings there was a great cheer and they all rose to their feet.

At the same time they heard three blasts of a trumpet.

'The Firbolgs are coming!' cried a man at the door.

How they hurried to get out of the hall! Swept along by the crowd, Eileen looked out for Seamus and the leprechaun. She felt something small and soft squeezing against her legs.

She glanced down, and there was the white pig!

There was such crowding about the doors that Eileen was afraid for the little creature. She stopped and picked up the white pig. It sat in her arms like a dog and grunted comfortably.

As she came out she saw Seamus in front. She called him, but he didn't hear. He was hurrying to get to the walls.

Eileen ran too, but the pig was heavy.

'You're a little nuisance,' she told it. 'There's going to be a battle. Maybe one that will be written about in the history books, and here am I, carrying a pig!'

But she could not put it down to be trampled on and, as the crowd began to spread out, she got nearer to the front.

There were steps leading up to the walls and many of the people mounted there. But the guards were opening the gates and armed men were marching out. Eileen saw Seamus with them and, tucking the pig under her arm, so that it wouldn't be noticed, she held her head up and marched too!

'Here! Take your weapon!' called someone, and a spear was thrust into her hand.

Eileen held it.

'If I meet Fuzzy I'll give him a whack with it!' she murmured. 'But if they think I'm going to stick it into anybody, well, I'm not!'

The white pig grunted.

'Maybe we'd be better on the walls. We'd see more!' said Eileen.

She turned to go back, but was pushed onward.

'Would you be a coward in face of the enemy?' asked a voice at her elbow.

'I do wish people wouldn't start calling names without any reason at all!' thought Eileen indignantly.

Darkness was creeping over the city and the hosts of the Danaan marched in silence. But away on the plain, near the river, the Firbolgs had lit a great bonfire, and they came rushing onwards, carrying flaming torches which flung their shadows on the grass and made each one seem many.

The chief of the Firbolgs strode in front and from all directions groups of the dark little men were hastening to join him. They were some distance away when the Danaans halted. Eileen heard a low word of command, and a shower of spears, which gleamed like stars, flashed through the night.

Eileen thought of Sreng and felt terribly unhappy. Then she saw that the spears had been flung so high that they passed right over the Firbolgs and fell into the river behind them without hurting one!

When the Firbolgs saw the spears coming they dropped flat on the ground, but when they discovered they weren't hurt they sprang up and came on, cheering and shouting.

Now they threw their great heavy spears. They didn't aim in the air but low down, so that they would be sure to hurt the Danaans.

But the Danaans lowered their shields and made them into a barricade. The thick, clumsy spears of the Firbolgs struck against them with a great thud, then dropped to the ground, bent and blunt!

'Now maybe they'll go away and leave us alone,' thought Eileen hopefully. 'I don't mind a fight if no one is hurt much!'

But the Firbolgs came on, chanting their war-song.

Eileen began to feel thankful that she had a spear and gripped it more tightly, when the pig under her arm gave a grunt and a kick, and there was the leprechaun beside her.

'Well, Eileen!' said he. 'We meet in strange places. I'm greatly obliged to you for minding me pig. I'll take him now.'

Eileen handed over the pig.

'We're going to charge!' the leprechaun told her. 'Run as fast as you can and hold your spear low!'

'If I stick this spear into anybody I'll never get over it!' declared Eileen. 'You take it and let me come behind you!'

'Indeed I won't!' replied the leprechaun indignantly. 'I don't need a great knife stuck on a stick to keep me safe. I trust to magic!'

'I wish I'd kept with Seamus,' sighed Eileen.

'Charge!' came the order.

Eileen ran, because if she hadn't she would have been knocked over and trampled underfoot. The Danaans were slow to fight, but when they were once started there weren't many who could stand against them.

Instead of holding her spear low, as the leprechaun had advised, Eileen put it up over her shoulder and gripped it in her two hands. As they reached the ranks of the Firbolgs she saw Fuzzy making straight for her. In one hand he held a sharp, two-edged sword, on the other arm he carried his round shield.

'I'll cut you in two!' he shouted, and raised his sword.

Eileen swung her spear and caught him such a whack with it that the sword was wrenched from Fuzzy's grasp and there he stood scared and disarmed.

On dashed Eileen. She was excited now and swung her spear from side to side so that she cleared a pathway right through the ranks of the Firbolgs.

In her white, shining tunic, the gleaming band about her hair, she looked very different from the child who had entered their camp in Sreng's company. She seemed so fearless that she terrified them and they gave way before her, so that at last she came right through their ranks.

When she found herself alone with the whole army of Firbolgs between her and her friends she lost her courage and was so frightened that she kept on running.

The river lay in front. She could go no farther. But a low bushy tree grew on a bit of rising ground and, laying down her spear, she climbed into the highest branch.

The bonfire made such a brilliant light that Eileen could see right over the plain.

The Firbolgs were losing! The dead and wounded were lying in heaps. Groups were still fighting, others were being chased to the river and many swam to safety on the other side.

Eileen looked sadly at the conflict. She wondered if Sreng had escaped.

Below her in the river there was a great splashing. Eileen glanced down, thinking it was caused by one of the Firbolgs.

To her surprise there was the Salmon of Wisdom.

'You are in danger there!' he gasped. 'If any of the Firbolgs find you they will kill you. Let me take you down the river where it is quiet and peaceful!'

22

The Firbolgs are defeated

 can't go without Seamus!' replied Eileen. 'Then there's the leprechaun and Sreng. I must say good-bye to them. Besides, I want to see what happens!'

'You are a silly little girl!' exclaimed the Salmon scornfully. 'I offer you a chance of safety and you won't take it. I've a good mind to splash you!'

'I can be safe nearly all the time!' replied Eileen. 'Besides, if I go with you it will be running away, and I'm not going to be the only coward in this fight!'

Just to show the Salmon of Wisdom that she meant what she said, Eileen jumped down from the tree and marched back the way she had come!

She did not get very far. A fighting crowd of Danaans and Firbolgs surged about a great rock which stuck up from the plain, and when she tried to get away from them a Firbolg rushed at her.

Eileen had forgotten her spear and now she was quite defenceless. She was too terrified to run, but as the Firbolg was almost on her she dodged. He turned and slipped, tripped over his spear and went sprawling on the ground!

Eileen crouched behind a boulder and lay there panting.

The struggling mass of men surged around her hiding-place. She covered her eyes to shut out the sight of warriors cutting and stabbing, but she could not shut her ears to the cries of pain and anger.

After a while the battle moved away from the rock, and Eileen, determined to find Seamus, crept out.

She gazed anxiously about her, when she heard a cry of pain and sorrow almost at her feet.

It was dark in the shadow of the rock and Eileen had to stoop down before she could find the wounded man.

Three lay there, the chief of the Firbolgs, a boy with his arms flung over his face, and another who moved and groaned.

The light from the bonfire flared up, scattering the shadow, and Eileen looked down upon Sreng of the Beeches!

With an effort she lifted his head. He was pale and he clenched his teeth with pain, but he managed to smile up at her.

'What shall I do?' she asked. 'Shall I bring anyone or shall I bind up your wounds and help you to escape?'

Before he could answer, someone touched her shoulder and, looking up, she saw Seamus.

How glad she was, for he too was unharmed, though he looked sad and tired.

'I've been searching everywhere for you!' he said. 'Oh, Eileen, I was terribly afraid you were hurt!'

'Sound the horn!' gasped Sreng. 'The chief is dead. Sound the horn and my poor followers will surrender. The Danaans will make peace. They are merciful!'

Seamus unfastened the horn which hung at Sreng's

belt and clambered swiftly up the steep rock. Eileen put the shield under Sreng's head so that he could rest more comfortably. Then she bent over the boy who lay beside him.

Gently she took his hands away from his face and sadly looked upon Fuzzy. Though he had been her enemy she knelt weeping beside him.

When Seamus reached the top of the rock he could see over the plain right to the gates of the city. The bonfire made by the Firbolgs was blazing away and made the whole place almost as bright as if the sun were shining.

He put the trumpet to his lips and blew.

Not a sound came, though Seamus puffed and puffed. Seamus took the trumpet from his lips and stared at it in amazement. Then he laughed. He had been blowing at the wrong end!

Once more Seamus blew. This time the shrill, harsh notes rang across the tumult of the fighting. Three times Seamus blew the trumpet of the Firbolgs. Then stood watching.

The Firbolgs knew the warning sound and shouted out their surrender. But when they raised their eyes to the summit of the rock and saw there a lad in the white, gleaming dress of the Danaans, they thought themselves betrayed and gave a great wail of anger and sorrow!

The Danaans, taking advantage of their confusion, seized their arms and took them prisoner.

The leader of the Danaans strode towards the rock and discovered Eileen standing beside Sreng.

'I make the same offer that your chief refused before,' he said. 'Let us share the land between us. Let there be peace between Danaans and Firbolgs. Ireland is our country and there is room for all!'

'I am willing!' replied Sreng. 'I know you are not really our enemies. And now all my people will agree!'

The Danaans lifted him on his shield and carried him to the great hall.

Holding Eileen's hand, Seamus marched behind the shield on which lay Sreng. He carried his spear over his shoulder and wondered if they would let him take it home with his beautiful shield.

'What will happen next?' Eileen asked herself.

They passed between the great bronze gates. The people of the city crowded to meet the victors and to gaze curiously at the Firbolg prisoners. But when they saw them vanquished and wounded they took off their bonds and led them away to bathe and rest.

In the banqueting hall they put down the shield and tied up Sreng's wounds, pouring such healing oils on them that soon he was able to sit up.

'We will build you and your people as fine a city as this,' said the leader of the Danaans. 'Then we shall dwell at peace with one another.'

'I am not chief of the Firbolgs,' replied Sreng. 'I was their leading warrior. But I do not care for the dull life of a chief. I like wandering, seeing strange people and countries, making new friends. Let the Firbolgs elect a new chief. Then I will go away with Eileen and Seamus!'

'But the children will stay with us!' said the tall man with the crown. 'Already the boy is a fine warrior. The girl is brave and clever. In a few years she will be our best singer!'

Eileen felt Seamus grip her hand. She knew he was tempted.

'We cannot stay!' declared Eileen. 'Our mother and father will be looking for us. If they never found us they would be terribly unhappy. So would we. Besides, this all happened long ago. You belong to the past. We must live in our own time!'

'You should not have said that!' whispered the leprechaun anxiously. 'Run! Or you are lost! You will belong neither to the past nor the present!'

Seamus made up his mind at once.

'Come along!' he cried sharply, pulling Eileen from the hall.

The flags, the banners, the great pillars, the lofty walls were growing dim. As they ran through the streets the houses were shrouded in mist, and the people who gazed at them in wonder were shadows.

At the gates the guards leaned on their spears dreaming, and the children passed without question.

'To the forest!' cried the leprechaun, as he ran beside them. 'You must return the way you came!'

'I came into the city!' objected Seamus. But the leprechaun urged him on.

'The city exists no longer!' he said. 'Make haste while the forest is still there!'

'We must cross the river!' cried Eileen. 'But look, how high it has risen!'

They hurried by the rock where Eileen had seen the Firbolg chief and Fuzzy. She could not see them now. The rock was like a cloud!

There was the river. How could they cross it? They ran along the bank, but the boats were gone!

'We must swim!' declared Seamus.

But the river was a torrent, foaming and surging. They watched it anxiously.

'Salmon of Wisdom! Help me now!' called Eileen.

His big cold eyes looked at her from the river.

'Too late!' gasped the Salmon of Wisdom. 'Too late!'

'We can't get across!' said Seamus. 'Let's rush back. I can be a warrior!'

'I want to go home!' replied Eileen. 'I like home better than anywhere else in the world!'

Behind them came a great trampling. They looked over their shoulders. His trunk aloft, his big ears flapping, his little eyes twinkling – on came the black elephant. Upon his back was perched Sreng, and leaning down, he pulled the leprechaun and the white pig up beside him.

'Up you get!' said the leprechaun to Eileen and Seamus. 'Here's one will get us through the flood. Though maybe 'tis too late indeed!'

Eileen gave a jump and scrambled up. Seamus hesitated. Through the mist, which grew thicker each moment, he heard the faint sound of a silver horn!

The leprechaun sighed. Sreng shook his head, but Eileen spoke to the elephant.

'Lift him up! Lift him up!'

The elephant's trunk twined round Seamus. Holding him high in the air he plunged into the river. The water rose about them. Uprooted trees swirled down on them, but the elephant carried his passengers safely to the other side.

Seating Seamus next to Eileen, the elephant strode on. They went by the deserted camp of the Firbolgs and entered the forest.

The trees were swaying and bending. Seamus could hardly keep his eyes open. Eileen's head was nodding. Sreng yawned loudly!

The leprechaun sprang to the ground. The white pig rolled after him. The black elephant shrank. Smaller and smaller he grew until Eileen, Seamus, and Sreng were sitting on the ground.

From the roots of the giant beech the leprechaun pulled out Eileen's leather coat. He buttoned it round her neck and gave Seamus and Sreng a sleeve each to hold.

'Leave something of the present behind. Take something of the past with you!' he told Eileen, who wasn't so sleepy as the others.

She pulled a handkerchief and pencil from her pocket, filling it with dried beech leaves. The leprechaun poked the handkerchief and the pencil into a hole in the tree.

'Jump over the roots!' he commanded.

Holding the sleeves of the leather coat, Seamus and Sreng jumped and Eileen with them. They were so tired that, though they thought they were leaping high in the air, their feet struck the roots which grew above the ground. Instead of tripping them the roots were so soft and yielding that they did not notice what had happened.

Splash! Thump!

Where were they?

They sprawled with outstretched arms and legs on hard wooden planks, only saved from rolling into the canal by the amazed turf-cutter, who dragged them out of harm's way.

There was the turf pile, and there the road to home.

They could see the whitewashed cabin at the edge of the bog and the blue turf-smoke rising from the chimney. In all the wonderful past they had not seen anything more lovely.

How it all began, or?

I have been asked to say something about how THE TURF-CUTTER'S DONKEY came to be written. This is difficult. It is always hard to explain how something grows. I had written a small book, THE COBBLER'S APPRENTICE, which had won a literary prize in Ireland. When a new daily paper started, I began writing a few short stories. These were run on like a serial and then I was asked to contribute a serial story, for children, to appear every day.

I sat at the upper window of my room overlooking the Dublin mountains and chewed the end of my pencil. How could it be done? I did not know. But I started, putting in all I knew and felt about life in Ireland, the whitewashed cabins on the bog, the happy family with the children, Eileen and Seamus, the little grey donkey whom the children called Long Ears, after they rescued him from the cruel tinkers, with their swaying caravans and their camp-fires in the dusk.

When I was fairly launched on my voyage into the Ireland of the present and the past, I found I had any amount of material to draw on. I wrote it from week to week. There were adventures as there always are to the adventurous. My story lasted for about three years. I had bundles of letters from children. One little servant girl who worked for an artist's family in Dublin, read my story as news and ran in to her mistress crying out excitedly that terrible things were happening in the country and no one was doing anything about it.

When, at last, the serial ended, I found I had written enough adventures not only for THE TURF-CUTTER'S DONKEY *but for two other Turf-Cutter books. I then wrote* LONG EARS – *a fourth – about the early life of the donkey before the tinkers had him and before he became the friend of Eileen and Seamus. When* THE TURF-CUTTER'S DONKEY *appeared, the Junior Book Club made it their selection. Since then the little Irish donkey has trotted over the roads in many countries. It has appeared in America and in various continental languages. The strangest edition I have seen is in the Malayan tongue, with the early Jack Yeats illustrations. Siobhan McKenna – our great Irish actress – did the narration when it was a serial on BBC Television.*

How did it come to be written? I haven't explained it because I don't really know. Those who have read UNCLE TOM S CABIN *will remember how when the woolly-headed Topsy was asked about her origin she said 'I spect I just growed!' The same is true about* THE TURF-CUTTER'S DONKEY.

Patricia Lynch